Of Course She Knew!

Just for you!

Millie Curtis

Millie Curtis

Avid Readers Publishing Group
Lakewood, California

Acknowledgements

Where would I be without friends and family to keep me on track? My thanks to Elizabeth Curtis Blye for listening, editing, and taking care of the computer glitches, and Amy Curtis Nishimoto for proof reading. To my husband of fifty-eight years, Fred Curtis, for editing and sending me back for a—gritting my teeth—rewrite. My lovely granddaughter, Anica Moran, who is, once again, my willing model for the cover. A rose to my friend, Pat Hepner, for providing information on Leadville, and to the ladies at the Clarke County Historical Museum for providing background on the early Berryville High School. Finally, a big thank you to Eric Patterson of Avid Readers Publishing Group for making it possible for me to publish another book.

This book is dedicated to my brother, Robert Charles Wilson, a proud U.S. Marine who showed his courage during the Korean War while enduring the Inchon Landing, the taking of Seoul, and surviving the Chosin Reservoir entrapment. Semper Fi!

Chapter 1

Adelaide Richards scraped a light film of frost off the small window of her loft bedroom in the tenant house she shared with her parents, two younger brothers and baby sister.

She pressed her lightly freckled nose against the glass and peered out onto the early spring morning where the sight of the Virginia countryside with green grass, budding trees and frisky baby lambs gave her a warm feeling.

Adelaide loved the springtime. It held promise. With her eighteenth birthday only weeks away, she would finish school, spend a busy summer, then go on to the State Normal School for Women down in Harrisonburg to become a teacher.

It was her mother who insisted that she get further schooling. "Don't get trapped, Addie," she had said. "You get something to support yourself." Was that how her mother felt? Trapped?

From below, she heard brisk movement in the kitchen. Smells of brewing coffee and frying bacon mingled together as they wafted their way up to where Adelaide knelt her appealing body at the round window. She heard the baby send up an ear-piercing yowl.

"Adelaide Mae, get down here and help with breakfast or feed the baby, I don't care which."

When her mother used both her names, and Adelaide hated them both, it meant there was no time to dally. She dropped the worn shawl covering her shoulders onto the bed, slipped on her drab dress, colored a mixture of mustard and pea green, and climbed down the ladder. She hated the dress as much as her name. As she only owned three dresses for school and the other two needed laundering, she had no choice.

A glass soda bottle with a rubber nipple stretched across the top held the baby's warm milk. Addie lifted the unhappy six-month old from her cradle.

Holding Sarah Jane in her arms, she went to sit in a rocking chair in the farthest corner of the room that served as a kitchen and living area. Adelaide's dread was that the smell of bacon would permeate her clothes. Wearing the ugly-colored dress was enough, she didn't want to smell like fried pig. The girls at school would be sure to make some unkind remark or whisper and cast a sly smile in her direction. If it wasn't for her good friend, Lottie Bell Foster, Addie thought she wouldn't have been able to tolerate school.

Lottie Bell lived on the same farm in another tenant house. The big farm sat outside the town of Berryville and had roots back to the family of George Washington. Both of their fathers were hired men. The owner of the farm provided housing and some portions of food so families stayed on. Trapped!

Adelaide's mother had grown up the same way. When John Richards came to work on the sprawling acreage, she quit school and they married when she was sixteen. Now, at thirty-four, she looked tired and worn. Perhaps she didn't want that for her daughter. Perhaps that is the reason she pushed Addie to get good grades in school and why she insisted that she become a teacher.

Addie looked over at her mother as she hurried about getting breakfast on the table for her husband and the two hired men who would come with him.

Was Mrs. Richards pretty when she was young? Addie tried to picture her mother as a girl her age. Laura Richards was tall and slim, taller than Adelaide, with chestnut colored hair and dark-brown eyes. If it wasn't for the dark circles under her eyes, the red roughness of her hands, and the lack of a ready smile, maybe she was pretty.

Adelaide's attention turned to the little sister she had helped bring into the world. She recalled the ordeal as though it were yesterday. She had just arrived home from school and was in the loft changing her clothes when she heard her mother groan.

"Are you all right, Momma?" she asked as she backed down the loft ladder. When she turned, her mother had a pained look on her face and there was a pool of liquid under her feet.

"My water's broke and this baby is coming fast. There's no time to run for help, Addie, you'll have to do it."

3

Adelaide shivered at the thought of how scared she had been.

After an hour of her mother's agonized groans and cries and instructions of what Addie needed to do, the baby arrived. Adelaide watched in wonder as the baby's head emerged followed quickly by the rest of her body covered with a cheesy film. Automatically, she picked up the squirmy, slippery, wet thing who cried the minute she landed. Adelaide feared she would drop the newborn, so she laid her on the sheet covering her mother's stomach.

"Tie a tight string around the cord about three inches from the baby's stomach and another string two inches from that. Be sure and tie them tight. Then cut the cord between the two strings," her mother panted out the order. "Mind Addie, you make sure they're knotted tight or she could bleed to death."

. Addie had washed her hands and poured boiling water over a sharp butcher knife. The string was strong crochet thread from her mother's mending basket.

Addie's hands shook as she remembered how she had been afraid to make the cut on that bluish, sinewy piece of pulsating material, but she did as ordered. She swaddled the baby in a small blanket and placed her in her mother's arms.

The mother's face contorted once again. "There's going to be afterbirth; get the big dishpan to put it in."

The terrified look on the daughter's face was not lost by the mother. "Don't be scared, Addie. You've watched plenty of animals give birth. It's pretty much the same."

Adelaide fled from the room and returned with the large pan. A big lump of bloody tissue, with one end of the severed cord attached, lay in the bed. She scooped it up in her bare hands, threw it into the basin and ran out the door to the hog pen where she dumped the mass in the pig trough. It was quickly devoured by grunting boars.

Her hands were covered with blood and there were big splotches of blood on her apron. Yanking it off, she doused it in a pail of cold well water before she scrubbed her hands and arms clean.

As Addie sat recalling the whole process of delivering a baby into the world, she resolved that the Normal School looked a whole lot better.

The baby finished her bottle as the men came into the house. Addie placed Sarah Jane back into her cradle before she went to help her mother serve breakfast.

She was pouring coffee into mugs when her brothers burst into the room. "Charlie says I have to go to school next year and he don't have to."

"How old are you, Chip?" asked his father, with a half-smile on his face.

"Ten."

"Then you got to go two more years. Charlie's 12. He can come work on the farm."

"Seems to me you'd want more for your boys," said their mother. She placed a platter of eggs and bacon on the table.

"They can learn farmin' and maybe someday have their own. Not like our Addie here. You've got a good brain, and your momma is stuck on you bein' a teacher. The money's there for you, where it ain't for the boys."

Adelaide knew she was smarter than her brothers and all they ever wanted was to be farmers. If her parents had managed to put money away for her, then she was obliged to do as her mother wanted.

Adelaide stood eating bacon wrapped in bread. "I've got to hurry if I want to catch Lottie Bell or she'll go on ahead without me. I hate to walk to school by myself. I've only got a few weeks and I can't wait."

"You keep your studies up," commanded her mother.

"Don't push too much, Laura," advised Addie's father. "You can be hard on the girl."

Laura Richards turned her back and busied herself at the stove.

When Addie caught up to Lottie Bell, she was almost at the end of the lane that led onto the main road into the town of Berryville.

"I don't know why you can't wait for me," said a harried Adelaide.

Lottie Bell was unconcerned. "I don't like to hurry," she replied. "You smell like bacon."

"I had to help with breakfast. Do you think the smell will go away if I leave my coat open? You know those girls at school. They're sure to make some remark and cause my face to burn."

Lottie Bell was short, plain, and pleasingly plump. Nothing seemed to rile her. "I don't know why you let those girls at school bother you. They're just jealous."

Addie transferred the books she was carrying to her other arm. "Jealous of what? They all have more than we do."

"You're smart and the boys like you."

Addie wasn't impressed. "There aren't any I care about."

"It's good you're going to be a teacher. Most of those women end up spinsters. Me? I hope to marry Sam just as soon as I finish school."

"You should want more out of life 'cause he'll never have anything. I don't understand why you're so crazy about him. He's too much of a show-off and wild-acting for my taste. Has he asked you to marry him?"

"No. I just hope he does."

Adelaide stopped. "Hold my books while I button up my coat. That cool breeze is going right through me. I can't help it if I smell greasy."

Lottie held Addie's books and waited while she tucked in her scarf and buttoned her wool coat. Then she tied loose shoe laces on her ankle-length brown leather boot.

"You're going to make us late, you know. I hate to walk into class late."

7

"Then we'll walk faster." Before Lottie could protest, "Yes, I know, you don't like to walk fast, either."

Lottie Bell smiled at her friend. "You're wound up like an eight-day clock."

Addie apologized, "I'm sorry if I'm a bit huffy. I had to feed Sarah Jane and help with breakfast before I could leave the house. Plus, I have to wear this ugly dress."

Her friend was unsympathetic. "I hate this one, too. We'll be finished sewing the dresses we had to make for homemaking class next week. I say, once we're finished with school, we should have a party and burn these sorry duds."

Adelaide perked up. "Oh, Lottie. What a great idea! I should have thought of that. Look, here comes Mr. Miller in his buggy. Maybe he'll give us a lift into town."

"He's a sulky old man. He'll just go right on by."

Adelaide wasn't shy. She stepped into the road and waved him to a stop before she flashed her brightest smile. "Mr. Miller, we're running behind for school. Would you be so kind as to give us a ride?"

His answer was a nod of his shaggy head and a thrust of his thumb toward the back of the carriage. Adelaide and Lottie were quick to hop onto the back seat before he changed his mind. Not a word was spoken until the conveyance stopped in front of the Bank of Clarke County.

"Far as I go." His tone was final.

"Thank you, sir," came Addie's sprite reply. And the girls hurried off to the red brick building on Academy Street.

**

That afternoon Adelaide finished washing some soiled clothes and carried the pan outside to throw away the wash water. She had no sooner tossed the water onto the ground when she heard the sound of horses' hooves pounding over a small rise near the house. She watched as the black-clad fox hunters approached and thundered by.

Adelaide turned to go back into the house when she saw a hunter whirl from the pack and come riding toward her. She was glued to the spot. The robust rider reined in his horse and sprang from the saddle.

"Addie Richards! Is that you?" He grabbed her up into a bear hug and spun her around, with the empty washbasin still in her hand. Then he set her back on her feet. "It's me, Clay Lockwood. It's good to be home. You don't know how much I've missed this place."

Adelaide hadn't seen Clayton Lockwood for almost eight years. They used to play together when her mother went up to help with housekeeping at the big house. Then he went away to boarding school and spent summers with his grandparents on the Eastern Shore.

Adelaide was in awe. It was almost unbelievable that he was the same clumsy, chubby little boy she had spent hours with in play. He stood about six feet tall with dark brown hair that fringed under his riding helmet. His bronzed face was clean shaven, his physique was that of an athlete.

Taken aback by his exuberance, she blurted out, "I didn't recognize you. You're not so fat."

"That's a fine greeting." He flashed a wide grin before he stood back and gave her an overall glance. "You have certainly changed from our days of hide and seek."

Laura Richards had been hanging laundry on the clothesline. She came to where the two young people stood. "Hello, Clayton. I hadn't heard that you were coming home. I'm sure your parents are pleased to have you here."

"Mother is deliriously happy. One is never sure of Father's thoughts." He mounted his horse. "May I come by after dinner? Addie and I have a lot of catching up to do."

Laura Richards gave her daughter a hard look. "Adelaide will be busy." She turned on her heel and went toward the house.

"Your mother doesn't seem pleased that I'm back." He leaned over from the saddle and whispered. "Meet me in the stables after dinner."

Addie gasped. "I couldn't do that."

He persisted. "Come on. I want to talk to you. How about tomorrow?"

"I don't know. I don't want Momma to get mad."

"She doesn't have to know."

Addie felt a pang of guilt and a sense of excitement as she answered, "Maybe tomorrow. I have to go to the big house to pick up goods my mother asked Johnathan to bring from the feed store."

"That's perfect. You have to go right by the stables on your way. What time will you be there?"

"I don't know." Adelaide hesitated. "With my mom acting the way she did, I'd have to be careful."

"I'll be at the stables all morning. See you when you get there." He swung his horse around and galloped to catch the other riders.

Addie was quiet as she entered the house. Mrs. Richards was standing by the fireplace with her back to her daughter. "You're not a little girl anymore. You and Clayton are from two different worlds and you'd better keep that in mind."

"He only wants to talk to me, Momma. Why'd you have to be so mean to him?"

"He's always been spoiled and pampered and I don't expect that's changed. It was okay when you were young, but I don't think the Lockwoods would relish the idea of him coming to see you." Laura Richards moved to the stove and stirred the stew with a finality that Adelaide recognized as an end to the subject.

Addie climbed up to the loft and straightened up the space she used as a bedroom. She had made a decision. Whether her mother approved or not, she would meet Clayton Lockwood at the stables tomorrow morning.

Chapter 2

A horse-drawn cart was hitched up for Addie to bring home the goods on the list her mother handed her with the command, "There's a passel of work we need to get done today so you hurry on back."

"Sometimes I have to wait if Johnathan hasn't sorted them out."

Laura Richards looked straight at Adelaide. "Mind what I said."

"Yes, Momma."

The boys were waiting when she came out of the house. "Can we ride up?"

"No. Pa says you've got to finish the chores he gave you." That wasn't the truth but the boys didn't know it.

"You're just bein' mean, Addie."

She was concerned her mother would hear them quibbling and make her take the boys. Without delay, she hopped up onto the cart and gave the horse a healthy tap with the reins leaving the boys behind.

On the way, Adelaide's stomach began to churn. Was it due to the thought of meeting with Clay or, more likely, the fact that she might be deceiving her mother? As she wasn't forbidden to talk to him, it wasn't being dishonest...or was it?

Fifteen minutes later, Addie arrived at the back of the big house. Josie Crim ran out to meet her.

"Mornin' Adelaide. We ain't seen you here in quite a spell. Yer gettin' better lookin' every day."

"My mother sent me up to get supplies Johnathan was bringing from the feed store. I spied him out by the shed. I'll go help him load them."

"He's comin' by here and he don't need no help. You get on in here and tell Mary and an' me what you been up to."

With mild reluctance, Adelaide climbed down from the cart seat and followed the scrawny little woman into the kitchen where Mary Jenkins was almost up to her elbows in bread dough.

The chunky, jovial Mary gave Adelaide a wide smile. "Addie, my love, it's good to see you. Get on over here and give me a peck on the cheek."

"Hi, Mary," she said as she kissed the cook's rosy, plump cheek.

"Just where have you been, child? We wuz just sayin' the other day that we ain't seen you around, weren't we Josie?"

Josie sat at the table sorting dry beans. She nodded in agreement.

"I've been busy with my school studies and helping Momma with the baby."

Mary shook her head. "Yer ma is a hard worker. I don't know why she lets you fool around with them books. Yer old enough to start yer own family."

"Not me," Addie responded. "I want more out of life than raising babies and doing housework."

Josie laughed. "So what are you gonna' do, Miss Uppity."

Adelaide defended herself. "I'm not uppity. I'm going to school to become a teacher and there is nothing wrong with that. Momma says she has money put away for me to go."

Mary and Josie exchanged a knowing glance.

Mary was busy shaping the loaves of dough. "Did you know that Clayton is back?"

"Yes, he came riding by the house yesterday with the hunters. I didn't recognize him because he's changed. He looked nice in his riding outfit."

"They all look nice in their ridin' outfits," opined Josie. "It's what's inside that counts, an' I 'spect he's as spoilt as he ever was."

"That's to be expected," said Mary. "He's one of them late-in-life babies. Now, you take Alex. He was my favorite."

"Alex? Who is he?" asked Adelaide.

"Ain't you never met Alex?" Josie piped up. "He's one of the Lockwoods. What do you think, Mary? Ain't he a good fifteen years older than Clayton?"

Mary stood back from her work and started counting on her doughy fingers. "Let's see.

Carleton's the oldest, then they lost that little one, then Alex. I 'spect yer right, Josie."

"I think it is strange that Clay never talked about him," mused Adelaide.

"Not so unlikely, Addie. Alex was sent off to boarding school and then went down to that William and Mary College. He's a lawyer down in Richmond."

"Well, I still think it's odd that I've never heard of him."

Josie pulled out a rotten bean and threw it into another bowl. "What's odd is that he's back after bein' gone fer so many years."

Mary nodded her head toward Adelaide. "Pull out a chair an' have a cup of tea with us while Johnathan loads them things he brought from town."

"Thanks, Mary, but I've got to be on my way. I'll try to stop by after school is over." She liked Josie and Mary, but they liked to gossip, and, if she met Clay at the stables and they saw her, it wouldn't do to be the brunt of an errant tale.

Outside, Johnathan was transferring goods from his big wagon to the cart she had driven up. He had worked on the farm for years and they showed on his lined face and stooped back. He was lifting a big sack of potatoes from the bed of the cart.

"Johnathan, let me help you with that."

"No, I got it. The rest of the stuff yer ma wanted is all loaded in. Some of the seeds won't be in fer a couple weeks."

15

"I'm sorry I wasn't here to help. Mary and Josie kept me talking."

"They's good at that. Where you been Miss Addie? I swear you look a lot like your momma when she was yer age."

"Was Momma pretty?"

"Pretty as a picture, she was. 'specially when she was out ridin'. Put all them fancy riders to shame."

Her mother rode horses? Adelaide was getting all kinds of surprising news.

"You be sure and tell yer momma that I asked about her. She and that new baby doin' well?"

"Yes. She doesn't get much time to rest with all the housework. I help as much as I can but I have to go to school and spend time on my studies in the evenings."

"You keep learnin', Miss Addie. I can see now why that's important. There's goin' to be more chances for women other than bein' stuck slavin' over a hot stove."

"I'm surprised to hear you say that. Josie and Mary think I should be starting a family."

He snorted. "I'm older and wiser than them two so you listen to me and yer momma, young lady." He gave a shy smile as he offered his coarse hand and helped her up into the cart.

"Thank you, Johnathan. It is always good to see you."

She headed back toward home but detoured on a side lane that led to the stables.

Clay was outside polishing a saddle. He raised his hand in greeting before he wiped it off with a rag and walked toward her as she climbed from the seat.

"I like to polish my own saddle and that stuff is smelly," he apologized. "I'm glad you came."

"I can't stay but a few minutes. My mother will be looking for me to help at home. One reason I wanted to come was to tell you I was sorry the way my mother acted yesterday."

He inclined his head with a slight smile. "And, what's another reason?"

Addie knew she was blushing so she was forthright. "I wanted to see you. You're a lot different."

"I can say the same for you," he observed. "Come on in and see the new foal that arrived early this morning."

They walked inside the stable where they leaned over a half-door to look into the stall. A spindly-legged, roan colt was struggling to get up.

"They're like babies." said Addie. "Not much to look at when they're first born."

She turned to look at Clay. "Why are you home now?"

"Home until I go to Mr. Jefferson's university down in Charlottesville."

"When will that be?"

"Not until the last of August. What about you, Addie? Are you still in school? I thought you might be off and married by now."

"My mother wouldn't allow it. She insists that I go to the State Normal School to become a teacher. Besides, I haven't seen anyone I wanted to marry."

"How do you feel about it? Do you want to be a teacher?"

"I guess."

They turned away from the stall to view a few more horses. Two boxes away a man stood currying his horse. They stopped to watch and he looked up from his work.

"Alex, this is Adelaide Richards. She lives in the little house over the rise."

The brothers did not look alike. Alex was an average looking man, trim and shorter than Reggie with sandy-colored hair. What Adelaide noticed most was the warmth of his deep brown eyes as he looked directly into hers. "Good morning," he said.

"This is my brother, Alex."

"Good morning," was her reply.

"Adelaide came by to check out the new foal," Clay explained.

Alex offered a pleasant smile. "Nothing like a new foal to create excitement. I'm pleased to have met you, Adelaide," he said, and went back to the task of currying his horse.

The two young people turned away.

"I've got to get home. My mother will be looking for me."

Clay walked beside her as they went to the door. "I'm glad you came. Do you think I could come by this evening?"

"No," she answered, without an explanation. "Clay, why didn't you ever talk about Alex? I thought Carleton was the only brother you had."

"They're both old enough to be my father. I hardly know them as brothers. Alex went away to school when I was born. I guess his name never came up when we were playing around the farm."

She smiled. "We did have fun, didn't we?"

"Yes," he agreed. "I miss those days, but now they tell us we must get on with our lives."

He helped Adelaide up onto the seat of the cart. "I want to see you again, Addie."

"Maybe one of these days," she answered, and headed the horse toward her home.

When she arrived, her brothers were not in sight leaving her to unload the goods she had brought. As usual, her mother was working in the kitchen.

"Did Johnathan bring everything I wanted?"

"He said they didn't have some of the seeds you asked for at the feed store but they expect to have them in soon."

Adelaide set a sack of flour on the table. "Momma, do you know Alex Lockwood?"

Laura froze in her spot. "What makes you ask?"

"Josie and Mary told me he was home and then I met him at the…" She had given herself away.

Her mother turned with a stern look. "At the what?"

"At the stables," Addie answered with a downcast look.

"What were you doing at the stables? I sent you to get supplies. Were you going behind my back, Adelaide Mae?"

"I met Clayton there because I wanted to apologize for the way you treated him. He showed me a foal that was born this morning."

Laura Richards shook her finger. "You don't have to apologize for me. I told you to stay away from him."

"No, you didn't say that."

"You know very well what I meant. I'll say it in plain English; stay away from all the Lockwoods! Now, get busy and start putting this stuff away!"

Adelaide didn't think she'd ever seen her mother so angry. The reason wasn't clear, but she knew not to say another word.

Chapter 3

Two days later, Laura was out hoeing in the garden patch near the house when she saw a rider approach. She knew who it was and continued to dig the weeds.

He got off his horse. "Hello, Laura."

"Hello Alex," she answered and continued chopping into the ground.

"I met Adelaide a couple of days ago."

"She told me. Why are you back? You haven't been here for years."

He stood holding the reins in his hand. "There was no need to come here. I used to meet the family at my grandparents place on the Shore because it was closer to Richmond. They don't have it anymore, so I came home to touch base. I may set up a practice here."

He toed some soggy leaves and kicked them away. "Laura, this is far too late, but I came to say that I'm sorry."

She stopped hoeing and stood upright. "You have nothing to be sorry for, Alex, we were teenagers. Your parents did what was best for you."

"But, it wasn't right." His warm brown eyes smiled at her. "I guess it was puppy love."

She gave a deep sigh. "That was a long time ago. Things worked out. John Richards has been good to me."

""I'm glad to hear that. Adelaide is a lovely girl."

"Yes she is, and she is going to get the chance I never had." Offering a confession, she continued, "Alex, for a long time I resented both you and myself for our foolishness, but that passed. If you want to do the best for me, then I would appreciate it if you and Clayton will stay away. Addie will be graduating soon and she will spend the summer at my sister's place. I don't want anything to get in the way of the plans I have for her."

He let those words sink in. "I hope my coming hasn't opened up old wounds. I understand your concern with Clay being home. I'll have a talk with him. I am pleased to see you again, Laura." He placed his foot in the stirrup and twisted into the saddle.

She watched him ride away and fought back tears as she stabbed the hoe into the ground. Perhaps the old wounds weren't healed as well as she thought.

When Addie came home from school, her mother sent the boys outdoors and told Adelaide to have a seat at the kitchen table. "I need to talk to you before you go up and change your clothes."

With noticeable apprehension, Addie laid her books on the table and pulled out a chair.

"I'm not going to scold you. When you asked me if I knew Alex Lockwood, I didn't give you an answer because I wasn't sure what to say. Yes, I knew Alex well. He and I were a couple years apart and kind of grew up together. When we were teenagers we thought we were in love. His parents weren't pleased with our infatuation and sent him away. I was ordered to not see him again."

Addie was stunned!

Laura continued, "There was no reason to tell you this before, but, now that he's back, I felt you should hear it from me. He came by today and said he had met you. I asked that both he and Clayton stay away."

Addie sat with the shocked look still on her face.

Laura reached over and covered her daughter's hands with her own. "I know I've been hard on you at times, but it's only because I love you. I didn't want you to make the same mistakes I made."

At that moment, Adelaide Richards' world seemed to fall in on her. "It all adds up, Momma. Josie and Mary gave each other a strange look when I said there was money for me to go to school. The Lockwoods gave it to you, didn't they? A payoff to stay clear of Alex. That's like bribery and you took it."

"That's not true. I looked at that money as a way out. But, then your Pa came along. The money was put in the bank for when it was needed. When you were born, we both agreed that it would be for you."

Addie pulled her hands away. "Did you love Pa or was he just convenient?"

Laura raised her hand as if to slap her child but restrained herself. She sank back in her chair. "That's a hurtful thing to say, Adelaide. Maybe I was confused. Your Pa has always been a good man."

"May I go up and change my clothes?"

"Addie, I regret that we needed to have this talk. One day you will understand."

"I'm not sure I will ever understand," she retorted.

Addie picked up her books and climbed up to the loft. Certainly she knew it was better to get the story from her mother rather than have it piped down the gossip line, but Addie didn't want to hear it. And, her mother had not said that she loved Pa. Adelaide was devastated. Would her world ever seem right?

Chapter 4

"You're quiet today," said Lottie as they walked to school.

"My mother and I had a talk yesterday, and I'm still mad at her."

Lottie Bell snickered. "That's nothing new. Did you bring home a bad grade?"

Adelaide kicked a stone. "I would have told you if I did." She wasn't going to tell Lottie about her mother's fling with Alex Lockwood because that would be embarrassing. "Clayton Lockwood is back home and she has forbidden me to see him."

"I don't know Clayton Lockwood."

Addie was surprised until she remembered. "I forgot. You've only lived here five years. Clay is one of the Lockwoods' sons. He and I used to play together. He was ten when he left to go away to school."

"What's he like?" asked her friend.

Adelaide smiled at the thought. "When we were little he was kind of fat and clumsy. Momma said he was doted on and spoiled, but he was always nice to me."

"What's he like now? It's not like you to be upset about not seeing a boy, and why did your mother forbid you to see him?"

Lottie Bell Foster asked too many questions.

"For one thing, she thinks he's too good for me. For another, she said she doesn't want anything to get in the way of me going to Harrisonburg."

"Which means he's a whole lot more interesting than when he was a kid," surmised Lottie.

They were passing the Berryville Hotel and waved at Henry, the boy who was sweeping the sidewalk.

Addie continued, "Clay is tall and good looking. He was riding with a group out fox-hunting when he spied me throwing out a pan of dirty water."

"I'll bet you looked fetching."

"He wanted to come to the house but my mother said no, so I met him at the stables. He wants to see me again, and I want to see him."

Lottie was miffed. "Why didn't you tell me this yesterday? I am your best friend."

"Because it was yesterday that my mother absolutely forbid me to see him. If she hadn't been so unbending, I wouldn't have cared if he came around or not."

They passed Irene Butler's dress shop where the dour seamstress was displaying a dress in the window. They stopped to watch.

"That's a pretty dress," said Lottie.

"I'll bet it costs a lot. Look at the lace on the front and on the long sleeves. Do you think it's silk?"

"Probably not. The sun might fade the material. Miz' Butler wouldn't take a chance like that. She's too tight."

"Like a corkscrew," enjoined Addie.

They giggled at their private joke and hurried up Main Street.

School was becoming boring for Adelaide. She found herself daydreaming much of the time about what life could be like. Whenever she had a few extra cents, she bought a dime novel about the West. It sounded exciting. Wouldn't it be great if she could go out there and experience it for herself? The dreamy state would pass and she would come back to reality. Ahead of her lay more years of schooling: more reading, more writing, more arithmetic. Why did it have to be that way? Because her mother said so, that's why!

When school ended for the day it was raining steadily.

"We're going to be soaked by the time we get back home," observed Lottie.

"I don't think we have any choice," replied Adelaide. "It doesn't look like it's going to stop."

They protected their heads with their shawls and hurried down the front steps of the school when a covered buggy pulled up.

"Do you young ladies need a ride?" called the driver.

Addie gasped, "Clayton Lockwood!"

"Good. He'll take us all the way to the farm. I want to meet him."

"What if my mother finds out?"

"Who cares? Come on before we get any wetter."

They climbed up into the buggy with Addie sandwiched between Clayton and Lottie.

"Lottie, this is Clayton Lockwood. Clayton, my best friend, Lottie Bell Foster."

They nodded and smiled at each other.

"How did you know what time we got out of school?" asked Adelaide.

"I saw you two walking to school this morning and knew you weren't dressed for rain. I had to come into town this afternoon so I asked when school was out."

"We're glad you came along," said Lottie.

Addie sat next to him with their bodies touching and was unfamiliar with the feeling that tingled through her. "I'll get off at Lottie's house when we get back to the farm."

"Alex told me that your mother doesn't want me coming around."

Lottie nudged Addie's arm.

"I'm sorry, Clay. That's the way Momma feels."

"Do you want to stop at The Virginia House for a cup of cocoa and doughnuts? It'll warm you up," Clay offered.

"Thanks, but no," answered Adelaide. Lottie Bell gave her another poke with her elbow. Lottie was fond of doughnuts.

When they reached the farm, Clayton drove to Lottie's house first. Addie started to get up, but Clay took her hand. "I'll drop you off at your house," he said.

Lottie leaned forward to look over at him. "Thanks for the ride, Clayton. It was nice to meet you."

"And, I am glad to have met you. I hope to see you again."

"I have a feeling you will," said Lottie.

Adelaide shot her a disgusting look.

Lottie's tone was light. "See you tomorrow, Addie."

They watched her slog through the yard to the small white tenant house.

Adelaide moved over to where Lottie had sat.

"Clay, you can't take me home. My mother will forbid me to leave the house if she sees me riding with you."

"What has she got against me?"

"She has nothing against you. She says she made a mistake when she was young that ruined her life and she doesn't want me to make the same one."

Clay stopped the horse and looked at her. "You'll be eighteen next week and old enough to make your own decisions."

"How did you know it was my birthday?"

"Don't you remember? Mary Jenkins used to make you a little birthday cake and we would go to our secret place and eat it."

She smiled at the thought. "I had forgotten."

"I wonder if that lean-to is still standing?"

"I don't know. I never went out there after you left. I wouldn't feel comfortable out there by myself."

"After the grounds dry up, why don't we go out and see if the rickety thing has fallen in," he encouraged.

"You have a short memory. I am forbidden to see you."

He ignored her statement. "When do you finish school?"

"Next Friday is our last day. We graduate on Saturday."

"Good. On Sunday, we can meet out there and celebrate your being eighteen and both of us being through with schooling for the summer."

"You don't seem to understand, Clay. I can't go."

"If you really want to go, you can find a way."

Clayton Lockwood was persistent. Perhaps he was still the spoiled little boy who got his own way. Nonetheless, he had set the wheels turning in Addie's mind.

"Maybe there is a way. Lottie and I are going to have a bonfire and burn two ugly dresses we own. That lean-to is well away from any of the houses so it would be a perfect spot. If I can convince my mother that I'm going to Lottie's house to spend the afternoon, we could meet out there."

"I like your way of thinking."

"I don't. It's being devious. On the other hand, I think my mother is being unfair."

Clay tapped the horse with the reins and they continued on down the lane.

"Let me off before we go over the rise," she ordered.

"You're still going to get wet and muddy."

"If you want me to meet you next Sunday, you had better let me off."

He stopped the horse. "Do we have a date?"

"I'll be there at two o'clock if Lottie can get away."

"And, if she can't?"

"I'll be there anyway." She hugged her books and wrapped the shawl as tightly as she could before she ran up over the rise and down the wet path that led to home.

The house was warm and smelled of wood smoke. Her mother was at the stove, as usual.

"Better get out of those wet clothes," she said, without turning to look at her daughter. "Then get back down here and peel potatoes."

"Yes, Momma."

Chapter 5

Adelaide's birthday was two days before her graduation from high school. Her mother baked a cake and the family shared her favorite meal of pork chops, fried potatoes, green beans and cornbread. They sang happy birthday and her present was that she didn't have to clear the table or wash the dishes.

Lottie gave her a card with a four-leaf clover pressed in wax paper. "You can use this as a book mark for those Western books you read," she had said. "Maybe it will bring you luck."

Saturday of that week was the big day. The day of graduation and no more school. Addie and Lottie had made their white graduation dresses in homemaking class under the watchful eye of the teacher, who was a stickler for perfection. Lottie was more patient and skilled. For Addie, she often heard, "Tear out that seam and sew it properly, Miss Richards." Words that Addie wouldn't have to hear again.

Saturday, at two o'clock in the afternoon, marked the end of Berryville High School for Adelaide Mae Richards, Lottie Bell Foster, and the other twenty-six students in the class of 1915. Two young ladies graduating from high school when girls living in tenant houses rarely went past the fourth or fifth grade of school, if they went to school at all.

Mr. Coyner of the local dry goods store had donated the white cotton material and lace trim for those in need. That meant Adelaide and Lottie. The two friends proudly sat in long white dresses with high-necks and long sleeves trimmed in lace. They fit in comfortably with the rest of the ten young ladies who would receive their diplomas. The boys looked dapper in white shirts, ties, and knickers. What an impressive display of the young scholars of Berryville.

The salutatory address was given by Adelaide. When she went to deliver the short speech, she spied her mother in the audience with a genuine satisfied smile on her face. Addie wasn't sure she had ever seen her mother so pleased. A fleeting thought crossed her mind that she was to meet Clayton Lockwood the next day against her mother's wishes. The pride her mother displayed on this day would be shattered by her daughter's deception. Addie couldn't bear the thought. Clayton Lockwood would have to wait.

That evening was a happy one for both families. Mary, Josie and Johnathan, the hired help from the big house, came by for a picnic lunch under a big oak tree near the Richards' house. Mary brought a three-layer cake she had baked and decorated with both Addie's and Lottie's names on it.

Addie's present was a suitcase. "You'll need this when you go away to school," said her mother.

Lottie received a gold locket from her parents. Being an only child had its rewards. But, Mr. Foster had once owned his own business and lost it all to alcohol. It was better to come from her family than to have to worry about a father coming home drunk, thought Adelaide.

On Sunday, she stayed home. Clayton Lockwood had been put out of her mind until he showed up at her house on that evening. Addie was up in the loft when she heard a knock on the door. Her father answered it.

"Good evening, Mr. Richards." With slight embarrassment Clay removed his cap. "I would like to speak to Adelaide if she is home."

If John Richards was surprised, he didn't let on. "Of course she is, Clayton. Come on in."

"Thank you, no. I'll wait here."

Laura Richards hurried to the door. "Addie is busy."

Unaware or oblivious to his wife's earlier warning to Adelaide, her husband countered, "I'm sure she ain't so busy she can't come to say hello."

Addie had started down and was off the loft ladder in a flash.

"Hello, Clay."

"You young people might be easier talkin' outside," suggested John Richards.

"You stick close to the house," ordered her mother as she shot a disgruntled look in Clayton's direction.

Addie closed the door behind her and they sat on a wooden bench at the side of the house. "What are you doing here? You know my mother is not going to be pleased about you coming."

"Where were you today? I waited at the lean-to for two hours. You said you would be there."

"I changed my plans. I thought about how underhanded I was acting and I didn't like the feeling."

"You've got too much of a conscience. I brought you a graduation present," he said as he pulled a small wrapped box from his pocket.

She was silent as she opened the gaily wrapped gift. Inside was a pin with what appeared to be a locket dangling down. She held it up into the light coming from the kitchen window, opened the locket and was surprised to see a watch-face.

"You will need a watch to keep you on time for classes when you go down to Harrisonburg. The jeweler assured me that it would keep accurate time. That is if you remember to wind it once a day." His smile was warm.

Addie ran her fingers over the ornate casing and examined the piece of jewelry once more before she spoke, "I have never seen anything so beautiful. Clay, I am pleased with your thoughtfulness, but I can't accept it."

If she had clubbed him with a bat he couldn't have looked more hurt. "It's a gift. What do you mean you can't accept it?"

"Because it is far more expensive than anything my family could afford. And, it is a very personal gift."

"Of course it is, that's why I gave it to you."

"I have heard that young ladies are not supposed to accept personal gifts from a gentleman."

"It isn't an engagement ring, Adelaide. It is a graduation present. If you're trying to make me angry and run me off, you're getting close."

His unhappy expression caused reason to settle in. "Clayton, I am sorry. The watch is lovely and I will cherish it always. You have to understand that I cannot wear it in public until I get to school. I won't even tell Lottie. It will have to be a secret like our lean-to used to be."

A relaxing sigh was heard. "Then you do like it?"

She took his hand. "I certainly do. Thank you, Clay. Whenever I wear it, I'll think of you."

"That sounds final."

"It is. I won't be here. My mother is planning on sending me to live with my aunt down in Boyce this summer. Then I am supposed to go to Harrisonburg." She lifted her hand from his but he snatched it back.

"You don't sound overjoyed."

"I have been doing a lot of thinking. If I can get my plans to work out, I won't be going to my aunt's or to school, either."

He gave a questioning look. "What is going on behind that pleasing face?"

"I can't answer that, but I promise I will let you know if plans change."

He kissed the fingers of the hand he held. "I'm glad we came together again. Are you sure I can't come by before you do whatever it is you hope to do?"

She smiled as she pulled her hand away. "No, Clay. You know how my mother feels. I will give her disappointment, and I don't want to add more."

"Addie, you have piqued my interest."

"Don't think too much on it. Good evening, Clay. Thank you for my thoughtful and lovely graduation present."

They stood up from the bench. "You're welcome." He touched her cheek. "You haven't left yet."

Chapter 6

The sky was overcast when Adelaide awoke. She dressed in a hurry and straightened up her bedroom area before climbing down the ladder to hear what her mother had planned for her. It was a strange feeling not to have to hurry through breakfast and hustle off to school.

Her mother was spooning gruel to Sarah Jane. "You wash and dry the breakfast dishes and sweep the floor. We can't do wash today because it looks like rain."

That was welcome news. "I want to go over to Lottie's house today."

Her mother continued to spoon gruel into the baby's mouth. "You've got to be getting ready to go to your Aunt Lilly's."

"I don't see why I have to go there and spend my time taking care of her bratty kids."

"Because I told her you would. She'll pay you five dollars a week. You'll need it."

Addie was sweeping the wood floor. "What about going to Lottie's?"

Laura washed the baby's face and hands and placed her back into her cradle. "We can't do the wash or hoe the garden if it rains so you might as well go on over. You get back here in time to pack your things for Lilly's and help with dinner."

"I wish we had an umbrella."

"Well, we don't. You can stay home. There are some socks that need darning."

That was all Addie needed to hear. She sat the broom on the back porch and pulled her shawl from a hook near the door. "I promise I'll be here in time."

On her way to Lottie's house Addie practiced how she was going to spring her idea on her good friend.

Lottie met her at the door. "I saw you coming down the lane."

"Can we go up to your room to talk?"

"Nobody's home. My mother went over to help Mrs. Jacobs before the baby comes and my father is out working on the farm. At least, I hope he is."

They went to the kitchen table. Lottie's house had the same room configuration as Addie's except there were narrow stairs leading up to two small bedrooms. Addie thought it would be nice to have real walls in a room instead of a loft where all the noise and smells wafted up.

"Do you want a cup of tea or a sandwich?"

"I ate a sandwich on my way over, but I could use a cup of tea."

Lottie began preparing the tea while Adelaide took a seat at the table.

"Do you want hot or cold tea?"

"I doesn't matter to me."

"It does to me. There's cold tea in the icebox. All I have to do is pour it."

Addie made a prune-face. "Then give me the cold tea. Lottie, how would you like to go to Colorado?"

Her friend almost dropped the glass she had taken from the cupboard. "Are you trying to be funny?"

"No, I'm being serious. Let's you and me go. I've been reading a lot and there's a place called Leadville that is a big mining town and there are a lot of jobs."

"How do you know that?" asked Lottie.

"Because my father got a letter from a friend of his. His friend wanted him to come out there and work for the mining company he works for."

"I'm putting a couple of cookies on a plate. Is your dad going?"

"No. He said he'd end up with a bad chest, and who wants to work under the ground?"

Lottie stopped what she was doing and looked at her friend. "I don't want a job. I want to get married."

"You said Sam hasn't asked you."

"He hasn't but I'm hoping he will."

"Finish with the tea and I'll tell you my plan."

"It'll have to be awful good."

Lottie brought the tea to the table along with a plate of sugar cookies.

Addie spilled her plan. "I've been thinking that I'm not keen on going to school to become a teacher. I don't want to take care of my cousins either, but my mother says that Aunt Lilly will pay me five dollars a week. If I work for the summer, I'll have fifty dollars saved up. That will pay for a train ticket and money to get a room until I get paid from a job."

"I don't have fifty dollars," said Lottie.

"You can get a job in town for the summer. And"…here was what Addie thought would be the clincher for Lottie to agree… "we'll go for a year. Sam will miss you so much that he will be ready to marry you as soon as we get back."

Lottie settled into her chair. "How long have you been thinking about this?"

"For a while. I want to do something exciting in my life before I have to settle down. I look at my mother and I know she wanted more than four kids and housework from morning to night."

Lottie sat quietly sipping her tea.

"I know. My mom doesn't seem all that happy either."

Addie didn't push.

"Do you think I could get a job in town?"

"Lottie you are an excellent seamstress and good with numbers. I'll bet either Mr. Coyner or Miss Butler would give you a job."

"You make it sound exciting, but we don't know anything about the West. You've been reading too many of those dime novels."

Addie leaned in close to her friend. "I read newspapers and magazines, too. Come on, Lottie."

"Why don't you go by yourself?"

"Because young women aren't supposed to travel alone and it would be better if we pool our money."

Lottie smiled. "In other words, you're not brave enough to go by yourself."

Dejectedly, Adelaide sat back in the chair. "It was just an idea I had."

Lottie hesitated. "Well... I think it's a good one."

Addie sprang to life. "You do?"

"This is the best chance we'll ever have if we're going to be able to tell a story to our grandchildren."

Adelaide sprang out of her chair and ran to hug her friend. "Let's not tell anyone. I'll go down to Boyce and take care of Aunt Lilly's kids and you get a job. We'll be ready to go at the end of August."

A clap of thunder sounded.

"The rain is getting close. I'd better get on home before I get drenched." She hugged Lottie again. "I'm so happy. This will be an adventure."

Lottie smiled. "Let's hope it's a good one. If we don't go we'll never know what it could have been. And, we're only going for a year, promise?"

"I promise. We can always come home before that if we have to."

Addie ran to her house and arrived just as a ferocious thunder and lightning storm hit.

"You're back earlier than I expected," was her mother's greeting.

"I need to get my things ready to take to Aunt Lilly's."

Her mother looked up from folding a blanket. "You're awfully chipper. You didn't go behind my back and meet up with that Clayton Lockwood, did you? It was bold of him to come to the house."

"No, Momma. I went over to Lottie's just as I said I would. When Clay came by the other evening I told him that he isn't to come around anymore because you don't want him to."

"Good," said her mother and went back to her task.

Adelaide climbed up into the loft and sorted out what she needed to pack for the summer. She didn't have much, so the ugly mustard dress that she and Lottie didn't get around to put in a bonfire went into her suitcase. Whatever she packed would also be what she would take to Colorado. Who knows? They might need those distasteful dresses.

Laura Richards's reception when Addie returned home had dampened her enthusiasm but not enough to squelch the zeal she felt for what lay ahead.

Chapter 7

The reluctant trip to Aunt Lilly's meant an outing for the whole family. It was six miles to Boyce, which seemed to take forever in the farm wagon with two horses pulling it. The weather was comfortably warm.

Aunt Lilly's husband owned a sheep farm and was a wool buyer, which made them considerably better off than the Richards family. The farmers sold their wool to him and he, in turn, sold the wool to the company buyers.

The Pierce place sat back about a quarter mile from the main road just south of town. It was a two-story wood farmhouse with plenty of room and a big porch across the front. A small stream ran next to the long drive up to the house. For Adelaide the one luxury would be her own room.

Lilly's features were a close resemblance to her older sister, Laura. The two held private conversations out of earshot of the children. Since her aunt's disposition wasn't any sunnier than her mother's, Addie wondered if Aunt Lilly had lost her supposedly true love as her mother had, or was that the way it was once a woman married?

Uncle Frank, Aunt Lilly's husband, was a big man. He was rough handling the animals and strict with the help, so Addie kept her distance.

Most of time he was out working on the farm and that was fine with Adelaide.

As for the children she was to care for, they ranged in ages from infant to eight. The two oldest girls, Emily and Flossie, were only a year apart. They quibbled and tattled on each other as often as they could. Aunt Lilly differed from her sister when it came to discipline. Her method of correcting her daughters was to say, "You girls be good." Of course that mild reprimand was ignored by the spiteful pair while Aunt Lilly went on about her business.

The nine-month-old, Carroll Joseph, whom they called CJ, had not been a healthy baby since he was born. CJ needed a lot of attention. Addie was to take care of the girls and help with housework.

When the Richards arrived at the farm, John and Frank went to tour the farm and talk about whatever farmers talk about.

Lilly made a fuss over Sarah Jane, exclaimed how everyone had grown and took Laura into the house where they settled in the kitchen to put a big dinner on the table.

Adelaide's brothers ran out to explore the place while Addie, followed by the two girls, went to her assigned room off the parlor to put her things away.

"Momma put clean sheets on your bed, Addie."

"That's nice. I like clean sheets."

"I helped her."

"You did not, Flossie."

"I did, too."

"I'm gonna' tell Momma you lied."

45

"Hold it girls," ordered Adelaide. "We're not going to have any of that kind of behavior. There's not going to be any whining or tattling. If you want, you can help me unpack my suitcase."

That suggestion calmed the girls, eager to see what the case contained. Addie put the suitcase on the bed. She lifted the latch on the hinged lid by pressing a button, bringing a squeal of delight from the captivated onlookers.

The wooden case was covered with tightly woven wool material of a dull brown with metal corner guards and a leather handle. Addie pulled up the hinged lid and fully opened the case.

Blond and blue-eyed Flossie reached in and grabbed a hand mirror.

"I'm gonna' tell Momma on you. You're not supposed to touch other people's things."

"Emily, I don't care if Flossie holds my mirror as long as she is careful with it." Addie turned to Flossie. "Emily is right. You are not to touch other people's things without first asking their permission. You may put the mirror over on top of the dresser along with my hairbrush and comb."

Adelaide pulled clothes from the suitcase and piled them on the bed. "Now, Emily." She pointed to a wall of the room. "You can take the books out of the bottom and put them over in that cubbyhole. I think they will fit right fine."

Emily, the older of the two with brown hair and large, round, brown eyes was a contrast to her sister's coloring. She eagerly went about the task she was given.

Adelaide put her toothbrush and can of tooth powder next to a wash basin on the dry sink. She picked up a bottle of rose-scented toilet water. "Come over here you two and I'll squirt you with this to make you smell sweet."

They bounced to their cousin's side.

"We're going to have fun with you here, aren't we, Addie?" exclaimed Flossie.

Adelaide wasn't so sure.

Dinner was served at a long oak table in the dining room. The girls, pushing and shoving each other, argued about which one would sit next to Addie.

"Girls!"

The tone of Uncle Frank's voice was enough to silence everyone.

Adelaide split the awkward moment with a suggestion. "You two may sit on either side of me, if it is all right with your parents,"

"Go ahead," came the gruff permission from Uncle Frank. "Lilly, you'd better get a handle on keeping those two in line."

Aunt Lilly shared a tired look with her sister.

Yes, to Adelaide it looked like it was going to be a long summer.

**

Two weeks later, Addie received a note from Lottie who was working at Irene Butler's dress shop. She wrote that she didn't like working

47

for the cranky sourpuss, but, if she could stand it, she would have fifty dollars saved by the end of summer. It wasn't all bad because she was learning from the knowledgeable seamstress. Perhaps her sewing skills would help secure a position once the two friends landed in Leadville.

Lottie also related that good-looking Clay Lockwood had given her a ride into town one day and asked about Adelaide. Of course she told him Addie was at her aunt's home.

Of course she did. And, what else did Lottie tell him, wondered Addie.

Chapter 8

Addie didn't have to wonder too long about what Lottie had told Clay. The next afternoon he rode up the hard-packed dirt driveway of the Pierce home.

Adelaide was outdoors supervising Emily and Flossie taking turns on a big swing that hung from a long rope. She felt her heart thud when she recognized the rider.

He spotted the small group and turned his horse toward where she stood.

"Who's that comin', Addie?" asked Emily.

"He's a friend."

"I wanna' get off the swing," shouted Flossie.

Adelaide slowed the swing to a stop as Clay dismounted. He threw the reins back over the horse's neck and allowed the horse to graze.

"Hi, Addie." How nonchalant could he be?

She tried to mimic his cool manner although her heart was pumping away. "Hello, Clay. What are you doing here?"

"I came to see you. Who are these two pretty little girls?"

Emily and Flossie turned shy, a rarity for them.

"These are my cousins. Girls, this is Mister Clay."

He squatted his large frame down to where he was eye-level. "I'm sure you have names. Let me see," he paused before pointing to Emily. "You must be Snow White and your sister is Cinderella."

The girls giggled.

"My name is Emily and this is Flossie."

"Why don't you two get your dolls and show them to Mister Clay?" suggested Adelaide.

Without delay they ran to the house to bring their treasures for the stranger to admire.

"A clever ploy, Miss Addie." His smile relayed his pleasure to see her again.

"You shouldn't have come."

"I thought it over. Your uncle deals with my father so I was sure he wouldn't run me off. Can't we go someplace to be alone?"

"No. I am busy with the children."

Clay Lockwood sat on a bench under the oak tree that held the swing. "I'm sure your aunt and uncle would allow you go over to the store for some soda."

Addie stood holding onto the long rope. "I'm not going to ask."

"I'll ask."

He was beyond belief. "You are persistent, Clay. If you recall, I didn't invite you. I know Aunt Lilly is going to tell my mother."

He gave a half-hearted smile. "What difference does that make? Wait until she hears that you don't plan on going down to the normal school."

Addie's mouth gaped. "Lottie told you!"

"Sure she did. Don't worry, I'm not going to tell anyone. Your secret is safe with me."

"I'm not sure I like you."

He stood up and took her hand. "Of course you do."

She pulled her hand away as the girls came running from the house.

He was right, but she wasn't going to let him know how she felt. Her mother's words rang in her ears. "He has always been pampered and spoiled and I don't expect that's changed".

The girls slowed their pace as they neared Clay.

He sported a wide grin. "Come over here and introduce me to your dolls."

Addie joined them to bolster their courage. "Emily, you may tell about your doll first."

This pleased Emily. She held up her prized possession dressed in a red velvet long dress and matching bonnet.

"Why, she's almost as pretty as you," remarked Clay. "Does she have a name?"

"I call her Betty."

"That's a very nice name for her. What about your doll, Flossie?"

"Her name is Joanie. See, she's got a scar where her face melted because I got too close to the fireplace."

"Did she cry?"

Flossie laughed. "You silly. She isn't real."

"Flossie, that wasn't nice to call Mister Clay, silly," admonished Adelaide.

"I'm gonna' tell Momma," warned Emily.

Clay laughed. "There's no need to tell your mother. I was being silly. Do you think your momma would let us all go and get a bottle of pop at the store?"

The threat of tattling was quickly replaced by the mention of pop.

Adelaide wagged her head. "You do have a way with you, Mr. Lockwood. You had better come to the house and meet my aunt."

Aunt Lilly, with her back to the door, was in the kitchen holding CJ. She turned at the sound of their approach.

"The little one just woke up from his nap, Addie." A look of surprise appeared on her face. "I didn't know you had a visitor, Adelaide." Flustered, she smoothed her apron.

"Aunt Lilly, this is Clayton Lockwood, a friend of mine."

He nodded. "I am pleased to meet you, Mrs. Pierce. I apologize for my unexpected visit. As I was in the area, I decided to stop by. I've offered to take Addie and the girls for refreshment over at Green's store. That is, if we have your permission. Perhaps you would like to accompany us."

Addie smiled to herself knowing he was bending the truth to his satisfaction. Was Aunt Lilly gullible enough to accept his explanation?

"That's fine. I know the girls would love to go. I need to feed CJ. You all go right on ahead. I do thank you for the invitation."

That was it? No warning, no lecture, no cross looks? Aunt Lilly was more understanding than Addie's mother.

"Can we bring our dolls?" asked Flossie.

Adelaide took her wide-brimmed straw hat from a hook by the door. "No. You'd better leave the dolls here."

Not one whining complaint from either of them. The band of four bid goodbye to Lilly and headed down the drive.

"Do you think the girls will get tired?" asked Clay.

"It's less than a mile," answered Adelaide. "We can stop and rest if we have to. The walk will do them good so they will sleep well tonight."

Emily and Flossie skipped on ahead.

As they walked down the road, Clay said, "It's good to see you, Adelaide. I've seen your friend Lottie a couple of times. Do you think you've planned well? I mean about your idea of going to Colorado? It isn't just a whim?"

"Lottie and I have talked it all over. We are going for a year. Maybe, if we like it, we'll stay there."

"Maybe you'll wish you'd gone to become a teacher."

She sent a wry look in his direction. "You're beginning to sound like my mother."

"Just a thought. Let's not spoil the day."

By the time they got to the store on the main street of the town, the girls skipping had turned to lagging.

"We're tired, Addie."

"That's what you get for hurrying on ahead. Come sit on this bench while Mister Clay and I buy the pop. What kind do you want?"

The girls took seats on the bench at the side of the store.

"Flossie wants ginger ale and I want root beer."

Once inside the store, the clerk pried the tops off the four sodas. "Those are the little Pierce girls out there, aren't they?"

"Yes," answered Adelaide. "I'm their cousin helping out Aunt Lilly."

"Here's a bag of popcorn to go along with those drinks."

"We only planned on getting pop," advised Addie.

"There's no charge. You tell Lilly and Frank I said hello."

Adelaide picked up the bag of popcorn and two of the drinks while Clay handed over his money.

"Thank you, sir," he said to the storekeeper. "The girls will be happy."

Clay, Addie, Emily, and Flossie crowded together on the bench sharing the bag of popcorn.

"Addie, is Mister Clay your boyfriend?" asked Flossie.

Clay grinned.

"No, he isn't. He is just a friend."

"He could be your boyfriend, couldn't he?" Emily questioned.

Addie sighed. "He could be, but he isn't. Hurry up and drink your root beer because we have to start back."

"We're too tired," informed Emily.

"Look, you two were all for coming to get a soda. We have to walk back home unless you want to sleep on this bench tonight."

That possibility caught their attention. Mopey looks turned worried.

"I have a solution," offered Clay. "I will carry one of you piggyback for a ways and then the other can have a ride."

This suggestion sparked new life and brought happy smiles.

"I want to be first and Flossie can be next."

"That's not fair, I want to be first."

Adelaide turned to Clay. "Do you see why I wasn't thrilled about spending my summer this way?"

He nodded his agreement.

"Let's do this," Addie suggested. "Flossie doesn't weigh much so I will carry her piggyback and Mister Clay can carry Emily. But, when we get to the farm, you will both have to walk up the drive."

That plan seemed satisfactory. Clay took the bottles back to the clerk. "The popcorn was well received by all of us. Thanks again."

Once he returned to the waiting trio, Clay and Adelaide hoisted the girls on their backs and started for home.

When they reached the long drive leading up to the house, both girls got down from their rides without a fuss as long as each could hold onto Mister Clay's hand.

"I wish a bigger girl would like to hold my hand," he chided.

Addie smiled.

Clay had put his horse inside a small fenced area so it could graze and drink water from a trough.

He leaned down to talk to Emily and Flossie. "I certainly enjoyed my visit today. I'd like to come back and visit again."

They clapped their hands.

"Girls, thank Mister Clay, then run in and tell your mother about what a good time we had."

A quick thank you and off they went.

"How about it, Addie? May I have the pleasure of your company again?"

Perhaps her next words were unkind, but she knew no other way. "Clay, you know the answer. You shouldn't have come today. If you don't respect my wishes, I will have Aunt Lilly tell you to leave if you come again."

"Didn't you have a good time?"

"That's not the point."

"Adelaide Richards, you're breaking my heart. I will give you your wish and not return."

Without further word, he leaped into the saddle and rode away.

Addie wasn't prepared for the instant feeling of loss that crept over her as she watched him leave. Yet, she knew that was the way it had to be.

That evening, after she settled the girls and CJ into bed, she came downstairs to say goodnight to Aunt Lilly, who was doing some mending.

"Clayton seems to be a nice young man, Addie. I do remember him from years ago when I visited at your place. Does your mother approve of him?"

"He is one of the reasons that Momma insisted I come here for the summer. He isn't a boyfriend, Aunt Lilly. We used to play together and he was always nice to me. We had a lot of fun times."

Lilly set her mending aside. "I have to be truthful, Adelaide. Your momma did tell me that because Clayton was back she was afraid he might get in the way of you going on to school."

"Momma worries too much. Just because she fell for someone out of her class doesn't mean I will."

"Adelaide Mae! Your mother was deeply hurt. You shouldn't talk like that."

"I'm sorry, Aunt Lilly. I feel like Momma wants me to live the life she wanted. I'm eighteen. I think I should be allowed to choose what I want. All I know is this county, and I would like to see how others in this country live."

Lilly sat for a moment before a weak smile appeared on her face. "When I was your age I felt the same way. There was no place to go, so I got

57

married. Young girls have more opportunity today, Addie. Don't let your dreams die."

This was a surprise statement. Would her Aunt Lilly approve of her plans? The temptation was to confide in her aunt, but it was too soon.

"I asked Clay to stay away. I told him he could write to me if he wanted to. He will be going to Charlottesville when the university starts."

"I believe that was a wise decision on your part, although the girls won't be pleased if he doesn't return."

"Yes, I know. I'm off to bed." She kissed her aunt's cheek.

Adelaide lay awake thinking over the day. She liked Clay. Although others saw him as someone who wants to have his own way, Addie saw him in a different light. He had always been kind and gentle and considerate. She saw his bravado as a façade, his way of fitting into his station in life.

Weariness crept in to blot out her thoughts, Adelaide Mae Richards fell fast asleep.

Chapter 9

Clay Lockwood had galloped away from Addie in a huff. He was down the pike a short distance before he slowed the horse to a leisurely gait. Addie Richards did not have a right to be so hardhearted. Or did she? As his hurt feelings cooled to a simmer, he was able to bring himself around to acknowledge his part in the unpleasant encounter. Of course he was at fault. It was a selfish act going to the Pierce house unannounced. He wanted to see Addie, and they did have a pleasant afternoon. Rethinking the situation gave him some solace that his uninvited visit wasn't such a bad decision after all.

One of the traits Clay liked about Adelaide was her kindness. She had never laughed when he tripped over his own feet, or when he bumped into objects, or when he spilled his drink. No, Addie had always been kind. Not like the girls he was forced to dance with at the cotillion dances. He was clumsy and they let him know it. More than once his face had burned with embarrassment. By the time he was in his senior year in school, he had grown into his bigness. No longer the awkward kid, he had turned into the agile athlete. The thought made him smile. Those same girls who had caused his agony tried to gain his favor, but he ignored them.

His mind churned as he rode toward Berryville. School would start in another month. It wasn't his choice to struggle over more books, although it was a necessary step. He would have to make something out of his life. He wasn't sure what.

His thoughts turned back to Addie. What would she be doing while he was studying at the university? Being foolhardy, that's what she would be doing, she and Lottie. Maybe he could convince Lottie not to go to Colorado. Addie would have to stay home and go to school like she should. All he would have to do is get that obnoxious hired hand, Sam, to ask Lottie to marry him. That wouldn't work for two reasons: Lottie, although lacking in the looks department, was a nice girl and deserved better than Sam, and because the news of his interfering would get to Addie and she would never speak to him again.

Clay rode on. The best thing to do is to let Adelaide go on with her plans. As long as he had her address he could write to her. Maybe she will get homesick and return after a few weeks. Maybe she won't get homesick and will want to stay there for the rest of her life. The thought made him kick his horse into a trot and on into Berryville he went.

Chapter 10

As summer wore on, Addie eagerly looked for it to end. She helped with all the household chores as well as took full care of the girls.

Aunt Lilly cared for CJ. The little one was thin and pale. Aunt Lilly thought she should take him to Berryville to see Dr. Hawthorne. But when she suggested it, Uncle Frank barked out, "There's no need to pay good money just because he looks puny."

Addie thought Aunt Lilly should take CJ to the doctor no matter what Uncle Frank said, but her aunt was not one to upset the apple cart, which in this case was Uncle Frank.

Why her aunt married her uncle was a mystery to Adelaide. She found little to like about him. To her it seemed his only aim in life was to make money. If there was a caring bone in his body, he kept it well concealed. She was beginning to realize why the girls acted as they did and why her mother insisted she come to help. With Aunt Lilly having to spend so much energy on their little brother, the girls' need for attention was ignored. Once she realized the situation, Addie began to see Emily and Flossie in a new light.

There was a small brick structure near the house that was no longer being used as a garden house. Adelaide got permission from Uncle Frank to use it as a playhouse.

"Go ahead," he had said. "It ain't good for much else."

With help from Emily and Flossie, they pulled out broken pots, old sticks and leaves, and swept the uneven wood floor. Then they scrubbed the place by hand until it smelled clean.

"Can we put up a curtain at the little window?" asked Emily. "I think that would look nice."

"First, we need some furniture," said Adelaide. "Let's go out to the barn to see if we can find something."

What they found was a half-used can of whitewash. "Look girls, if we can use this, we can paint our little house and make it brighter inside."

One of the hired men was in the barn.

"Could we have this? We want to paint the inside of the girls' playhouse."

Adelaide's query posed a quandary for the man. "I don' know. Frank's pretty tight with his stuff." He scratched his head. "I ain't fer sure he knows this is left over from the job we did. I guess if it's fer his girls, I 'spect you can use it."

Addie didn't wait for him to change his mind. "Come on girls, let's go find some paintbrushes."

It was a hot July day and hotter inside the little brick garden house. Adelaide found a good-sized brush for herself but none for the girls. She painted everything inside, including the old wood floor. The girls were allowed to take turns painting the step in front of the playhouse.

"We'll leave the door open so it will dry quicker," she advised them. "It should be dry enough that we can use it tomorrow."

"We need curtains," reminded Emily.

"Tomorrow, we'll work on them and try to find something for furniture. Right now, Emily, you and I will get some oatmeal cookies and a jug of water while Flossie gets that "Mother Goose" book we were reading."

Fifteen minutes later they were sitting on the bench under the oak tree enjoying oatmeal cookies and reciting nursery rhymes; a happy trio waiting for the paint to dry in their newly acquired playhouse.

"Addie, why didn't Mr. Clay come back to visit?" asked Flossie.

"Because he's busy working on the big farm where he lives."

Emily shook her head. "Uh, uh. Momma said you told him not to visit anymore."

"Why did your momma say that?"

"I told her that Flossie and I wanted him to come back again and she said he wouldn't be coming."

"Your momma is right and so am I. He does work on his father's farm." The girls didn't need to know that his work was polishing his own saddle and exercising his horse.

"Let's get Momma and show her how we painted the garden house," suggested Flossie.

Addie was relieved to have the conversation shifted from Clay Lockwood. "Yes, let's," she agreed. "Emily, you carry the water jug and Flossie, you carry the book."

"What are you going to carry, Addie?"

She gave each a kiss on the cheek. "I'm going to carry myself. Let's see who can walk to the house the fastest."

Lilly was sitting on the wide front porch rocking CJ.

"Momma, come see how we've fixed up the playhouse," entreated both girls.

"I can't come right now. I'm holding the baby."

"Aunt Lilly, I'll hold CJ while you go out with the girls. They will be disappointed if you don't."

"He's about to drift off to sleep."

"If he does, I'll place him in his cradle."

Having successfully circumvented her aunt's protests, what else could Lilly do but follow her excited daughters to view the transformed garden house.

Addie was happy to have the quiet solitude of rocking to and fro. As the little one drifted off into a deep slumber, Addie's mind drifted off to her friend, Lottie. She hadn't received a letter from her in almost three weeks. Lottie had better not be getting cold feet about going to Colorado, thought Addie. She had better not!

Chapter 11

They were on their way to the village of Boyce for groceries. Adelaide drove the wagon while Emily and Flossie sat in the bed and Aunt Lilly, with CJ on her lap, sat next to Addie.

In the weeks she had lived at the Pierce home, Addie had grown fond of her aunt, who was more understanding of Addie's feelings than her own mother. Addie wished her aunt would buck Uncle Frank and take CJ to see Doctor Hawthorne because he seemed to be punier than when she first arrived. Perhaps today was the perfect opportunity to voice her concern.

"Aunt Lilly, I heard you say that you would like to take the baby to the doctor. I can drive you over to Berryville if you want."

Lilly's reaction caused Addie to pull the wagon to a halt. Lilly broke into tears, muffling her sobs in the baby's blanket so the girls wouldn't hear.

Addie put her arm around her aunt's shoulder. "I didn't mean to upset you. I only meant that he doesn't seem to be gaining as he should."

"I'm sorry. Your words brought to light what I've known and have chosen to push aside. I know you're right, Adelaide, but Frank says there is nothing wrong with his boy."

Addie gasped. Was Frank Pierce blind? After a moment's hesitation she found her courage. "There is no question. Aunt Lilly, whether Uncle Frank allows it or not, we are taking the baby to see Doctor Hawthorne. We can drive into Berryville and get back here before dinner."

"I wouldn't dare go against Frank's wishes."

"I would. You need to have an answer. This must be eating your heart away."

Addie turned the horse-drawn wagon north. Uncle Frank may kick her out of the house when they returned, but she didn't care as long as her aunt got an answer about her child.

Forty minutes later they arrived in the town of Berryville. Everything looked the same, although Addie felt as though she had been away a long time. They drove up the main street of town past the hotel, the barber shop, the dress shop to where the huge red brick Hawthorne House was as imposing as ever. Addie pulled the wagon to a spot along the street and tied the horse's reins around a substantial tree.

"Aunt Lilly, I'll take the girls with me. I want to see my friend who works in Miss Butler's dress shop, and then I'll buy the girls some candy at Mr. White's store."

Lilly handed CJ to Addie while she climbed down from the wagon. "If I don't see you at the doctor's office, I'll come back here and wait for you."

Emily and Flossie were more than happy to go with Adelaide.

"Is it true, Addie? Are you going to buy us candy?"

"Yes, as long as you behave yourselves in Miss Butler's shop. You can't touch anything or talk loud. I don't think Miss Butler likes children to come into her store." Addie wasn't sure if Irene Butler even liked children.

The dress shop was a few doors east on Main Street. Luck was with Addie. Irene Butler had gone to the Battletown Inn for lunch. Lottie was tending the dress shop. When she saw Adelaide, she dropped her sewing and hurried to meet her.

"Addie! I'm so glad to see you. What are you doing in town?"

"My aunt had to bring the baby in to see Doctor Hawthorne. These are my cousins, Emily and Flossie." She turned to the girls, "This is my friend, Lottie."

"Hello, girls. Is Addie being good to you?"

"She's going to buy us candy if we behave," informed Emily.

Lottie smiled. "I've got a piece of cake in the back room. You can share it if you want."

That satisfied the girls and removed them from the temptation of touching anything in the shop. It also gave Addie and Lottie a chance to talk.

They kept their voices confidential.

"You haven't changed your mind have you, Lottie?"

"Changed my mind about what?"

"You know. About going to Colorado."

"Why would I do that?"

"I haven't heard from you in weeks. I thought maybe Sam asked you to marry him and you jumped at the chance."

Lottie was flippant, "I gave up on Sam."

"Gave up on him? Why?"

"Clay talked me out of it. He said I was too nice a girl to get saddled with the likes of Sam."

Addie didn't care for the casual use of Clay's name.

"Have you been seeing Clay?"

"He's given me a ride into town a few times and we've gone to the cinema. He's right nice, Addie."

Clayton Lockwood and Lottie Bell Foster? A pang of irritation rippled through her body. Could it be that Adelaide was jealous?

It wouldn't do for Lottie to see any reaction. "I've checked on the trains we have to take. It will only be a little over twenty dollars to get to Leadville. If we each save fifty dollars, we should be able to rent a room and buy food until we get money from our jobs."

"What if we don't get jobs?"

"We will. My father's friend wrote that there are many places to work."

"In the mines, you said. I don't plan on being a miner."

"Don't be silly. Miners have to eat and buy goods. Are you getting cold feet, Lottie?"

Her friend didn't answer right away. "I'm not as crazy about leaving as you are. I like working here."

Addie was point blank. "Lottie, Clay Lockwood will be going to the university at the end of August. If he's the reason you're having second thoughts, you had better forget about him!"

Lottie allowed a wry smile to appear. "What are you getting so fired up about? That's not like you."

"I'm sorry. I'm worried that you won't come with me and time is getting close. I have to have your word that you haven't changed your mind."

Lottie placed her hand on Addie's arm. "No, I haven't changed my mind, and when Clay and I are together all he talks about is you. Does that make you feel better?"

Her moment of discontent passed. Addie offered an embarrassed smile. "I did sound like a ninny, didn't I?"

"Yes," agreed Lottie.

Addie called to her cousins, "Girls, if you've finished your cake, thank Miss Lottie and we'll be off to the general store."

They hurried to where she stood. "Thank you, Miss Lottie."

Addie headed for the door. "I'll send all the details in a letter. We'll leave from the train station here in town."

Lottie was apologetic. "I haven't told anyone except Clay. It seemed right to let him know, and he promised to keep it a secret. I'll tell my parents the

69

day before we are to leave. They will probably be overjoyed. They are always encouraging me to get out in the world."

"I wish it would be the same at my house. I'm not sure how my mother is going to accept it. I dread that encounter."

The trio was going out the door when the shop owner arrived.

"Hello, Miss Butler," said Addie. "I stopped by to see Lottie."

"Hello, Adelaide. Lottie, here, is a big help to me. I understand you're helping your Aunt Lilly."

"Yes, for the summer."

"You tell Lilly that I asked about her."

"I will."

Irene Butler being cordial? That was a change.

At the general store, the girls picked out Mary Jane candies. Their choice pleased Adelaide because the molasses and peanut butter treats would last until they got back home.

"Can we buy some candy for Momma?" asked Emily.

"I guess we could," replied Adelaide, although she hated to part with the money. "What do you think she would like?"

To her relief they didn't pick out a nickel candy bar.

"Momma likes root beer barrels," advised Flossie.

"Mr. White, how much are these?" Addie asked pointing to the candies in a wooden tub on the counter.

"They're three for a penny, Adelaide."

"That's perfect. I'd like three."

He put all the candies in the same small paper bag. "How is your summer?"

"It's fine. These are my cousins from Boyce. I'm helping my aunt."

"That would be your Aunt Lilly?"

"Yes."

"You give her my regards."

Addie nodded. She had forgotten that her mother and aunt had grown up in this town.

"Hear you're goin' down to Harrisonburg in the fall."

"Those are the plans," answered Adelaide. Did the whole town know? Of course they did.

Aunt Lilly was waiting at the wagon when Addie and the girls returned.

The girls were enthusiastic. "Momma, Addie bought you some candy," informed Emily.

"I told her you like root beer barrels," said Flossie.

"It was their idea, Aunt Lilly."

She offered a gracious smile. "How very kind of all of you."

Emily and Flossie climbed into the wagon, eager to start on their Mary Janes. Addie and Lilly climbed up onto the seat. CJ was awake and looking around.

Adelaide turned the wagon south. It took effort for her not to ask what the doctor had said.

They were almost out of town when Lilly said, "It was good we came. Doctor Hawthorne said I should have come earlier. CJ is anemic."

"What does that mean?" asked Adelaide.

"It means he has weak blood. That's why he looks pale and throws up sometimes. The doctor gave me a tonic for him. I am to stop nursing and start giving him cow's milk and grind up meat to feed him three times a day. Then I am supposed to take him back in two months."

"What if he isn't better?"

"Let's not think on that, Addie. If he doesn't improve, Doctor Hawthorne says he may have a weak heart."

Adelaide didn't ask any more questions. Aunt Lilly's tone of voice told her that a weak heart wasn't good.

When they reached home, Addie hurried to start supper. Uncle Frank would be cranky enough when he found out about the trip to the doctor he didn't need to be vexed over supper being late.

Adelaide fried up sausage, mashed potatoes and made gravy. Tomatoes and cucumbers were ripe from the garden so she sliced them and mixed in mayonnaise and dill.

At the supper table, Emily was the one who spilled the beans. "Addie took us to Berryville today and bought us candy."

Frank stopped eating and looked up. "You can get candy right over at the store."

"I took CJ to see the doctor," said Lilly.

The room grew quiet.

Frank Pierce put his fork down and eyed his wife. "What did he say?"

"That CJ has weak blood and I should have come sooner. He gave me some tonic for him. I will be giving him cow's milk from now on and grinding up beef to feed him."

Adelaide was prepared for a big explosion from her uncle, but there was none. "I told you there was nothing wrong with that boy. How much did it cost?"

"I don't know. I told Doctor Hawthorne you would be by to pay him. He said I can pay when I take CJ back in two months."

"I'll pay him when I go into Berryville tomorrow." Uncle Frank didn't say another word. He picked up his fork and went back to finishing his food.

Adelaide's sigh of relief was silent. She gave a sideways glance to Aunt Lilly who offered a modest smile. Perhaps her uncle was relieved to hear that his son just needed richer blood. Her aunt was wise to leave out what else Doctor Hawthorne had said.

Chapter 12

August was hot. Barn smells were rank and offensive to the nose. Addie took the girls to the stream that ran by the drive to cool their bare feet and wet their faces. The girls could go shoeless but Addie had to wear her laced shoes and cotton stockings. At the shallow run, she put them aside and hoisted her long skirt to her knees. Sometimes the girls became boisterous and splashed water all over. Addie didn't care. The cold water was a relief and their clothes would be dry by the time they reached the house.

The girls adored their older cousin. Addie played school and held teas in the transformed garden house. She read them bedtime stories and sang funny songs like *The Itsy-Bitsy spider* and *I'm a Little Teapot.* They played Hide and Seek and Blind man's Bluff. But all good things come to an end and summer was drawing to a close.

Addie lay awake in her bed. It was too hot to sleep. Her mind swirled with what was ahead. Emily and Flossie would start school next week and Adelaide would return home.

CJ seemed to be improving. He had more energy and wasn't as pale. Perhaps Dr. Hawthorne was right; it was weak blood and not a weak heart that caused the baby to look puny and ashen.

For Aunt Lilly's sake, Addie prayed that was the reason.

Clay Lockwood had not returned. In her heart she had wanted him to, but she knew it was best that he hadn't. Lottie had written a letter last week that was troubling. She said Sam had come around. If Lottie got back with Sam, she could back out of going to Colorado. Although she and Lottie were good friends, throwing Sam back into the mix might change Lottie's mind.

Laying in the darkness of the room Addie's thoughts turned to the stories of the West she had read. Zane Grey's novels were alive with the color and landscape of the western states. She had read of Wyatt Earp, Doc Holliday, Bat Masterson, Billy the Kid and all the rest of the noted gunfighters and outlaws. The West sounded wild and romantic and exciting. She wanted to experience it for herself.

Adelaide got out of bed and left her room. The open air might not seem as stifling. She sat in a rocker on the screened front porch hoping sleep would come. If the thoughts of her coming adventure were not enough to keep her awake, the thought of confronting her mother was gnawing at her. In four days she would return to Berryville. Her mother may be so upset with her that she would disown her. That had happened to one of the girls in school when she had run off with a carnival man. When she came back, her mother wouldn't let her back into the house. That was two years ago. The girl disappeared and no one knew where she went or what happened to her.

Is it possible that her mother would be so hard-hearted when she heard of Addie's plan? In the quiet of the night with only the sounds of the crickets and tree frogs, Adelaide was beginning to doubt herself. Maybe she should go down to that State Normal School for Women. She could become a teacher in four years and then head west. Four years. That might as well be forever. With these thoughts whirling in her brain, she drifted off to sleep.

"Addie, wake up." It took her a few seconds to realize it was Aunt Lilly shaking her shoulder. "Whatever are you doing out here on the porch?"

Addie yawned and stretched to bring herself awake. "It was so hot in my room, I had to leave."

"I don't blame you. Not much air stirs in that room." Lilly sat in the chair next to Adelaide. "You'll be going home in a few days, and we are going to miss having you here. You have been a great help to me and the girls."

"At times I thought summer would never pass. I guess it's time to start breakfast," said Adelaide.

"In a few minutes. Addie, the girls over-heard you talking with your friend at the dress shop. They said you talked about going someplace together."

Addie was annoyed. She had tried to keep the girls from hearing. But, now her aunt knew and she couldn't lie, so she said, "Lottie and I are going to Colorado. A friend of my father wrote that there are a lot of jobs out there. I want to do something before I have to settle down. It will take me four years to become a teacher and I'll be twenty-two."

Her aunt sent her a kindly smile. "And, that will make you an old woman?"

"I'm afraid that if I don't go now, I'll get trapped just like Momma and you and..." She stopped at the realization of what she had said.

Addie rushed from her chair and put her arms around her aunt. "I'm so sorry. I didn't mean that."

Lilly patted Addie's arm. "I know what you meant. That your mother and I didn't have the chance to do anything but get married and raise a family. And, you're right."

Addie stood back from the chair. "What do you think Momma is going to say when she finds out that I'm not going on to school?"

"She's going to be hurt, Adelaide. It is her dream."

"But it isn't mine."

Lilly rose from the chair. "Then you must follow your conscience. Addie, you will always have a home here."

Adelaide kissed her aunt on the cheek. "Thank you, Aunt Lilly. I pray that all goes well for you."

They left the porch to make breakfast for the family and hired men. It was a thankless job every morning to cook over a hot stove in the summer heat and clean up the grimy dishes that would be left. She wouldn't have to do that in Colorado.

Chapter 13

The day came when Addie was to leave the Pierce house and return to her home in Berryville. The girls were in school and disappointed they couldn't ride to the train station to watch her leave.

Uncle Frank drove her to the Boyce station where she would take the 9:12 Norfolk and Western train to Berryville. To her surprise, Frank handed her a twenty dollar bill. "Adelaide, here's something extra for your help this summer. I know Lilly and the girls were happy you were here. Sometimes I may seem gruff but that's just the way I am. You make your momma and daddy proud down there in Harrisonburg."

Why did he have to say that? She was feeling guilty enough.

"I appreciate the extra money, Uncle Frank, and thank you for the ride. It was a good summer." That wasn't entirely true, although it did afford her the opportunity to raise the money to leave home. This extra twenty dollars was like insurance.

Frank had also bought her ticket. She decided to wait outside the station. Addie wore the ugly mustard colored dress that she despised, but it was a good choice for a smoky train ride. Trains always felt gritty. Her wide-brimmed straw hat kept the eastern sun out of her eyes as she sat on a bench in front of the attractive station paid for by local citizenry. Most towns had small station houses, but when the train company showed the plans of what they wanted to build, the local gentry turned them down and raised money to buy a larger more ornate station complete with electric lights and running water.

The train arrived on time. Adelaide carried her suitcase to the edge of the concrete platform where a porter guided her up the iron steps to board the railcar. There were a few unoccupied seats. Addie chose to sit in a seat next to an older lady. It was only a six-mile ride. If the lady proved to be talkative, she would only have to endure the conversation for a short time. It was better than sitting next to an older man. They were always clearing their throats or smelled of cigarette smoke or worse yet, smelled like they hadn't taken a bath in months.

"Do you mind if I sit here?" Adelaide asked of the woman.

The passenger glanced up from the magazine she was reading. "The train doesn't belong to me. You can sit wherever you choose." She went back to reading her magazine and never said another word.

When the train reached Berryville, Addie picked up her suitcase and stepped down two iron steps to the wood platform. She was back home. Her parents didn't know she was coming so there was no one to meet her.

Addie headed east from the railroad tracks. The people working in the milling company building were busy as she walked by in the direction of the big farm just outside town. She had walked that same road every school day but today it seemed longer and more tiring. She shifted her suitcase to her other hand when she heard a buggy coming behind her.

"Hey, Adelaide. Wait up," she heard a voice call.

She didn't turn around because she knew who that voice belonged to. She stopped short.

"Want a ride? That suitcase looks awful heavy,"

Addie looked at the driver who had pulled alongside her. "Hello, Clay. I don't have to ask how you knew I was coming today. You've been talking to Lottie."

"I had the buggy parked near the station, but you hustled off so fast I couldn't get the ornery thing turned around quick enough."

He got off the seat and took her suitcase before he gave her a hand up onto the seat.

Once he deposited the case in the back of the buggy, he climbed up beside her and tapped the horse with the reins.

"I won't say I'm not glad to see you because I am. The walk to the farm is tiring."

Clay cast a sly glance. "Is that the only reason?"

"I'm not going to answer that. Aren't you supposed to be off to Charlottesville?"

"That's next week, unless I decide to go to Colorado with you and Lottie."

Her mouth gaped. "What are you talking about?"

He chuckled, "Just wanted to see your reaction."

They left the road from town and turned left down the farm lane.

"Is your mother going to be upset that I've given you a ride?"

"Not as upset as when I tell her what my plans are."

"Addie are you sure you know what you're doing? You go down to Harrisonburg, I'll go down to Charlottesville and in four years we can both go to Colorado."

"No. I can go on to school next year. Clay, if I don't do this now, I never will. Have you ever seen the rules for teachers? They must put in ten-hour days, no keeping company with a gentleman except on Sunday, no tarrying in the stores, and they must be in their house by eight o'clock. No wonder they turn into Old Maids."

"I've heard of men sowing their wild oats, I never heard of a woman doing the same."

"Maybe it's time you did."

He laughed aloud.

When they reached the house, Clay reached for her hand before she could leave the seat. "Addie, you can write me at the University of Virginia, Charlottesville, in care of Clayton Lockwood. Write to me and let me know how things are going."

"I will."

"Promise?" he asked.

81

She smiled at the persistent young man sitting next to her.

"Promise."

Her brothers came running from the barn and her mother stepped out onto the porch holding Sarah Jane. Addie hopped out of the buggy and yanked her suitcase from the back before Clay could come around to help her.

In a quiet voice, he said, "Maybe I'll see you again before you leave."

"I doubt it," she answered.

Clay nodded to Laura Richards and waved to the boys as he turned the horse back toward the big house.

Addie met her mother on the porch.

"How'd he know you were coming?"

That was her mother's greeting, no: glad you're back, how was your summer, we missed you, no warm hug.

Addie kissed Sarah Jane on the forehead. "She's grown, Momma."

"Still a lot of work," said her mother. She turned and went back into the house.

Chip and Charlie came running onto the porch. "We got some new calves, and chickens, Addie. You want to come see them?"

She smiled at her younger brothers. "Not just yet. I need to unpack my suitcase. Want a peppermint stick?"

They each held out a grimy hand as she pulled the candies from her bag. "You ought to wash your hands."

"We'll hold onto the wrapper." Off they went in the direction of the barn.

Adelaide was sure Lottie Bell was working. If only she were home they could make final plans. Addie was eager to get everything in order so that nothing was left out. Afraid that last minute distractions could jeopardize their leaving, she climbed the ladder to the loft and wrote down every possible obstacle that could get in their way.

Sam was the biggest one. Even though Lottie said she was through with him, his name had resurfaced in letters Lottie had written to her.

Addie figured the sooner they left, the better it would be.

She hadn't decided when she would tell her mother. It wouldn't be tonight because she didn't want to ruin her homecoming.

"Addie, get down here and help me with the baby."

"I'm coming, Momma," she called down. Adelaide Richards was home, nothing had changed. To herself she murmured, "Yes, Momma, I am coming, and I am absolutely, definitely going!"

**

That night Laura Richards lay next to her husband in the darkness of the night. She could hear his easy breathing and sometimes a snore or two if he changed positions. John Richards had been a good husband to her and she had borne him four children.

When Adelaide arrived home today, Laura wanted to hug her tight and tell her how glad she was to have her home. But she had ridden home in that buggy with Clay Lockwood. Addie was as lively and carefree as she had been when she was in her teens.

Laura wondered what her life would have been like if Alex had remained on the farm. A few weeks ago when he came riding by as she was hoeing the garden, he had stirred thoughts she had buried so long ago. Alex wasn't handsome, but he had ways about him that pleased her. The way he stood easy holding the reins in his gentle hands, the slight cock of his head when he smiled. What upset her was the hurt in his warm, dark eyes and his words, "I guess it was puppy love."

She rolled onto her side. Why was she so hard on her daughter? Because she didn't want her to be hurt as she had been. She had seen the way Clay looked at Addie. Just as Alex had looked at her when she was young, vibrant, and pretty. Now she was tired. Tired from washing, cooking, cleaning, taking care of everyone's needs but her own. She wished she could be young again. She wanted to feel that excitement for tomorrow and what her future held. If only she could pile her hair up under a lovely hat, don a lace dress and dab some rouge on her cheeks maybe she could feel pretty again.

The tears started rolling down and she wiped them away with the sheet. Laura Richards hated this feeling of unhappiness. It was beginning to overtake her at all times of the day. This wouldn't happen to her Addie, she would see to that. Laura's Addie wouldn't get trapped.

At five o'clock, Sarah Jane cried and Laura dragged out of bed. If she had slept during the night, it wasn't for long. She opened the kitchen door to let the cool of the morning drift into the house. The air was already warm. Laura knew it would be a hot September day. After breakfast, when the men had gone, she would talk with Addie to be sure she was prepared to make the trip to Harrisonburg Friday morning. Laura had taken the money out of the bank to pay for school. What had Adelaide called it? A bribe? It probably was.

Addie had said she would go over to Lottie's house this morning and walk to town with her before her friend went to work at the dress shop. Adelaide wanted to buy a hat at Catherine Ramsburg's hat shop.

Laura was glad the two girls were going to part ways. In her eyes, Lottie was too crazy over that good-for-nothing Sam, who worked on the farm across the way. Addie had told her that Lottie wanted to marry him. Sam smoked and drank too much. So did Lottie's father. Mrs. Foster should see what a sad life lay ahead for her daughter and stop Sam from coming around, but she seemed to encourage it. It was good Addie wouldn't get mixed up in that mess, thought Laura.

Chapter 14

Addie donned an ankle-length cotton dress and climbed down from the loft to help with breakfast. Her mother was frying ham.

Laura didn't look up from her work. "Pop the biscuits into oven. It's hot."

"Momma, is it all right if I go to Lottie's without cleaning the dishes? I want to catch her before she goes on ahead."

"You can go. I want you to get back early because I need to talk to you."

Addie set the table and cracked a dozen eggs into a frying pan. She knew what her mother wanted to talk about. School. Adelaide was to be on her way to Harrisonburg in two days. She scrambled the eggs in the skillet with a whisk until they were cooked. Then removed them from the fire.

"The eggs are done. I'll leave them in the pan so they'll stay warm. I'm going on."

Laura nodded.

The men were coming in as Addie was going out. She was glad she didn't have to serve breakfast and clean up after them.

"Where are you off to in such a hurry?" asked her father.

"I'm going to catch up with Lottie."

"We just passed her. She's half-way down the lane."

"I'll run. Bye, Pa."

Lottie was almost on the road to town before Addie caught her.

"Wait up. I'm almost out of breath."

"I've got to be in the shop by eight or Miss Butler will give me a lecture."

"Have you told her you're leaving?"

"I didn't have to. She said she won't have enough work for me for the next couple months. Today is my last day."

"Lucky for us. I'll have to tell my parents tonight because we leave the day after tomorrow. It will cost each of us twenty dollars and a few cents to get all the way to Leadville. We have to take four different trains. All we will have to worry about is getting the right train."

Lottie sighed. "I wish that was all we had to be concerned about. The more I think about it, the scarier it sounds."

"Lottie, don't back out on me. Uncle Frank gave me twenty extra dollars. I promise that if you want to come right back home, I'll keep enough money for your ticket."

"That's generous. I guess you are primed to go."

"I can't wait!"

They walked up the main street of town, which was beginning to come alive.

"I'll go on up to the dress shop with you. Miss Ramsburg will have the millinery open on my way back," advised Adelaide.

"I hear she has a beau. Some rich man from Washington. At least that's what I overheard Mrs. Talley tell Miss Butler. They're always gossiping about what goes on in town."

They crossed Church Street and walked up to the dress shop. They had a few minutes to talk together on the sidewalk before the shop opened.

"Lottie, I'm going to buy a new hat and then I'm going to buy two tickets to Hagerstown for Thursday morning. The train leaves at eight-fifteen. You can pay me back."

"How do you think your momma is going to take this news?"

"I'll have to tell her when I get home. I have been dreading that encounter all summer."

Irene Butler unlocked the shop door. "You're early, Lottie. That's unusual for you. Hello, Adelaide."

"Good morning. We got an early start. I'm on my way to the millinery."

"Say hello to Miss Ramsburg for me. Well, get in here, Lottie. We have things to do."

Lottie sent a wry look in Addie's direction. "Yes, ma'am."

As Adelaide anticipated, the hat shop was open when she arrived. She climbed the short set of steps and opened the narrow door. A small bell tinkled.

Catherine Ramsburg came from the back room.

"Adelaide! How nice to see you. I've wanted to congratulate you for being salutatorian.

That was an accomplishment. I wish more young people would realize how important it is to get an education."

"Thank you. My mother drilled it into me."

"And wise she was. What can I help you with?"

At twenty-four, Addie had heard people say that Catherine Ramsburg was past her prime. Addie didn't think so.

With honey-brown hair, creamy complexion and a pleasing figure, Catherine Ramsburg was attractive. She was also friendly.

"I would like to buy a hat."

"We're almost into the fall season. I'd suggest a felt or wool. Here's one that would serve through the fall and winter." She held up a plain cloche hat in navy blue wool. This is a newer style and suitable for any color coat. Come and try it on."

"How much is it," asked Addie.

"Let's not worry about the price until you've tried it on."

With mild reluctance, Addie sat in the chair in front of a three-way mirror while Catherine fitted the hat. It was admirable from every angle.

"Addie, that is most attractive with your coloring. You can wear your hair up or down under this hat. To tell you the truth, I think this style is more for you younger set."

"It is lovely, but I came in to buy a straw hat."

"Let me see," said the milliner. "I believe I have a fall straw out in the back room."

She left Addie to admire her image in the mirror.

Catherine was back in seconds with a dark brown straw hat trimmed with a beige ribbon. She removed the cloche from Addie's head and popped the straw in its place.

"That's nice looking. The width of the brim complements your pretty hazel eyes and the light brown of your hair. The hats are equally appealing."

"Yes, I like them both, but I can only afford one."

"How much were you planning to spend?"

The question caught Addie off-guard. She might as well be truthful. "I can only afford two-dollars and fifty cents."

"That's perfect. Two-fifty will cover the cost of the two."

"Miss Ramsburg, they must cost more than that."

"The straw is a summer model and the wool has a slight blemish on the inside hat band." She pointed out a small dab of ink on the label.

"I can hardly see it."

"Nevertheless, it is a mark. You can consider it a present for doing well in school, if that makes you feel better."

"I can accept a present. I would love to have both of them."

Catherine got a hat box and placed the hats inside. "I hear you are going on to the Normal School."

"Unless plans change. Thank you, Miss Catherine."

Addie skipped down the steps onto the sidewalk. Her step was lighter as she headed toward home.

Clay Lockwood was waiting when she turned into the lane leading to the farm.

"Hi, Addie. I've been waiting for you."

"How did you know I walked into town?"

"Lottie told me you were going to. I saw her last evening."

Adelaide kept on walking. "You two seem to see each other frequently."

He walked beside her. "It's the only way I can keep tabs on you. Let's go sit on that log over there, unless you have to go right home."

"I can sit for a few minutes."

The log was a fallen tree in a copse of trees setting a short way from the lane.

"What's in your hat box? Hats?" He smiled at his own play on words.

"I bought them from Miss Ramsburg."

"I hear she's got a beau…"

"Some rich man from Washington," Addie finished his sentence. "I don't know. I didn't ask her. It's not my business."

"People like to talk."

"Gossip, you mean."

"Want to show me your hats?"

91

"Clay, I don't think you would be interested in my hats."

"Come on. Try them on. I want to see how pretty you look."

Addie placed the hat box on her lap and was opening the cover. "Don't laugh."

When she opened the box, Clay reached in and pulled out the straw. He held it up on his hand. "Tasteful," he remarked and placed it on her head. Then he leaned back to get a fuller view. "You look classy, Addie."

"Don't make fun of me."

"I'm not making fun of you. You are fetching in that hat."

Addie pulled out the navy cloche. "What do you think of this one? It's supposed to be a new style."

He took the brown straw hat from her head and placed it in the box. "Go ahead, try it on."

Addie did so.

He placed his large hand under her chin. "Turn your head to the left. Now turn it to the right. Look straight at me."

And when she did, he kissed her.

Addie's face turned crimson. "Clay Lockwood, that wasn't nice."

"I know, but you looked too pretty not to kiss. I should say I'm sorry, but I'm not."

Addie took the hat from her head and put it back in the box. She stood up from the log. "I've got to get home. I'll bet you planned that all morning."

"How was I to know you were going to buy hats?"

"If it wasn't hats it would have been some other devious trick. You Lockwoods are all alike."

He scrambled to his feet. "What do you mean by that?"

"Never mind. I've got to get home and tell my mother that Lottie and I are leaving on the Thursday morning train."

"Addie don't be sore. I've wanted to kiss you since I saw you throwing out that pan of dirty water."

That remark made her smile. "Clay, I'm not sore. And, I'm glad you kissed me. It's kind of a goodbye kiss."

"Want me to drive you to the train?"

"No. Momma would never forgive that. I promise I'll write to you at the university."

He took her hand as they walked down the lane. "Addie, all those years I was gone away to school, I used to think about the fun times we had. I missed the farm and you."

She squeezed his hand. "Those days are gone and we'll never get them back."

"Maybe there are good days ahead for us again."

"Maybe," she said. "Goodbye, Clay."

He kissed the fingers of the hand he held. "Bye, Addie. You keep yourself safe."

"I will," she agreed and went in the direction of the tenant house.

Chapter 15

"What did I hear you say?"

Addie repeated herself. "I'm not going to Harrisonburg."

Adelaide sat across from her mother at the kitchen table.

Laura Richards looked stunned as the words sunk in. The look on her face was a combination of disbelief and anger.

A threatening silence hung between them.

Addie quickly added, "Lottie and I are going to Colorado on Thursday. I've bought the train tickets."

Laura sat looking straight at her daughter causing Addie to fidget in her chair.

"Ever since Pa got that letter from his friend in Leadville, I've wanted to go. Lottie and I are going to get jobs out there. We'll come back if we don't like it."

Laura continued to stare at her daughter until she managed to say, "After all these years I've planned for you to go on to school to become a teacher and saved that money for you, you're going to throw it all away."

Addie stopped her nervous behavior and sat up straight. "That's just it, Momma. Becoming a teacher is not my dream, it's yours. You want me to live the life you wanted for yourself. I don't want that Lockwood money. Keep it for Sarah Jane. Maybe she'll be the teacher you dreamed of."

Laura Richards did not say another word. She rose from her chair in a trancelike state and walked out the kitchen door.

Addie collected her wits, ran from the house and caught up to her. "Momma, come back we need to talk about this."

Her mother turned with anguish in her eyes. "Leave me be, Adelaide."

Addie stopped and watched her mother walk out through the field. She hurried back into the house where her baby sister was crying. Addie swooped her up and rocked her in her arms. Fearful of the look in her mother's eyes, she said aloud, "What have I done!"

**

Laura Richards walked and walked oblivious to her surroundings. It was unlikely she would get lost because she had lived on this farm all her life. Growing tired, she found herself in the spot she loved best. She sat on the bank of the small stream that flowed through the farm and watched the clear water ripple over the stones at the sides and bottom of the run.

Laura's mind had been churning as she walked. At last she settled down to think and clear her thoughts. Addie's words had hit her with such force she was afraid of what she might do. All she could think of was to get out of the house before she physically struck her daughter or said words she would rue to her dying day. The encounter had been unraveling; all the plans she had made over the years for her daughter's future were gone.

"Laura, what are you doing way out here?"

The sound of a voice startled her. She turned her head to see Alex Lockwood walking over the rise.

Laura wiped tears from her eyes with the back of her hand. "How did you know I was out here?"

"I didn't. I was out checking fences because some cattle got out. I came to get a drink from the spring."

He sat on the bank beside her. "You look troubled."

"Family business."

"Can I help?"

"Not unless you can convince Adelaide to go on to the State Normal School."

He half-smiled. "Is that all? What is she going to do instead?"

"John received a letter from a friend in Colorado who says there are lots of job opportunities out there. She and that Foster girl are planning on going."

"And you don't approve?"

She cast a spiteful glance in his direction. "Of course I don't. I have always planned for her to become a teacher."

"It doesn't sound like that is what she wants."

Laura was irritated. "I know what's best for my daughter."

Alex pondered her words. "I don't know Adelaide well, but from what I have observed, she is a strong and independent young lady."

"Alex, I want her to make something of herself."

"And she will. She has a good head on her shoulders. You and John have been good parents to her. What does he think about this?"

"I'm sure he doesn't know. He says I'm hard on her because I have pushed her to get good grades in school. I want her to have more than I've had."

He shrugged a shoulder. "Maybe it's time you let go. You can't live her life for her or live yours over."

Her tone was scoffing. "When did you become so wise?"

"As I got out into the world. Your life isn't so bad, Laura. You have four beautiful children and a husband who loves you. What more do you want?"

Laura's demeanor changed. "Are you unhappy, Alex?"

He stood up. "Let's just say that I would like to have a wife and family rather than a law degree."

He offered her his hand and helped her up. "It's getting near suppertime. Don't you think you should be heading home? Your people are going to be worried."

She took his hand and rose to her feet before she heaved a heavy sigh. "I know. It's good that you came by. I believe you have made me look at this situation through Addie's eyes. "

He smiled. "Aren't lawyers supposed to be helpers? I've got some more fence to check before I get back."

She waved as they parted ways. "Bye, Alex."

When she reached the house, the family was eating supper that Addie had prepared. Laura walked into the room and everyone looked at her without a word being uttered.

Laura took her place at the table. "The food looks wonderful, Adelaide. It was good of you to prepare it."

John Richards looked at his wife. "Everything all right?"

She placed a helping of potatoes on her plate. "Everything is fine. Did Addie tell you she has changed her mind about going down to Harrisonburg? She and Lottie Bell are leaving for Colorado on Thursday morning."

"She told me. How does that set with you?"

Laura looked at Adelaide as she responded, "I was sorely disappointed. Sitting on the bank of the creek, I had a quiet place to think. I have come to realize that I wanted her to go on to school more than she did."

Then she said, "Addie, you are a bright and intelligent girl. I'm sure you have thought this through. So, I give you my blessing. Like you say, if it doesn't work out, you can always come back. When you were a little girl, if you heard that train whistle you would ask me where the train was going. Now, you'll find out."

Adelaide hopped out of her chair and hugged her mother around the neck. "Momma, I'm so glad you aren't mad. We were all worried about you."

"I know you were. It won't happen again. I took a long walk and did a lot of thinking." She patted Addie's arm. "We all love you, Adelaide."

Chapter 16

Addie hardly slept a wink Wednesday night. Her suitcase was packed, the train tickets were in her pocketbook, and she had packed a lunch to eat on the train. Feelings of excitement and doubt kept her awake. Her mother had said she could come back home if she needed. That was the safety net that kept her resolve to leave.

Adelaide was up early. The house was quiet. She was glad no one was stirring. Her father was already at work on the farm and her mother would be rising soon to fix breakfast.

Sarah Jane was asleep in her large cradle. Addie wanted to kiss her, but she knew that would wake the sleeping baby. Instead, she tried to fix the image in her mind of this beautiful little one she had helped bring into this world.

Her suitcase sat by the door where her brother had carried it down from the loft. Addie wore the ugly mustard-colored dress she loathed with the thought that she wouldn't have to worry about anyone taking a second glance at her. It would be bad enough that she and Lottie would look like they didn't know what they were doing, because they didn't.

Addie buttered two slices of bread for her breakfast, pinned the new brown straw hat in place, and picked up the heavy suitcase. Without anyone there to say goodbye, shed tears, or wish her well, she quietly left the only home she had ever known.

When she reached Lottie's house, Mrs. Foster was in the kitchen. Lottie was finishing her breakfast.

"Come on in, Adelaide," welcomed Mrs. Foster. "Would you care for a cup of coffee or a doughnut?"

The aroma of the hot coffee was enticing. It had been a cool walk in the early September air. "Thank you. I would like both. I left the house before my mother was up."

"Is she disappointed with your decision to not go to the State Normal School?"

"I think it broke her heart, Mrs. Foster. I'm not sure I want to be a teacher."

Addie took a seat at the table while Lottie's mother prepared the coffee and doughnut. "I see you're wearing your ugly gray dress, Lottie. It's good we didn't throw them into a bonfire."

Lottie had a mouthful of food. She nodded in reply.

Mrs. Foster placed her offerings in front of Adelaide. "I believe your mother will come around to see it your way. Lottie's father and I are pleased she has this opportunity to see more of the country."

"See Addie? I told you they would be glad to get rid of me."

Lottie's mother gave a playful tap on her daughter's shoulder. "Now Lottie, you know that isn't true. You are both bright girls and you need to gain some more knowledge before you settle down."

After they finished their breakfast, Mrs. Foster checked once more to be sure they had what they needed.

Adelaide Mae Richards and Lottie Bell Foster headed off to experience what lay outside their comfortable Clarke County.

Their suitcases were heavy. Because Lottie was plump and not as strong as Adelaide, she had to stop often to set hers down. To their surprise and elation they espied Clay Lockwood at the end of the farm lane waiting in a horse-drawn buggy.

He waved his cap as they neared. "You young ladies want a ride?"

Addie decided to act as casual as he did. "It depends on where you're headed."

He laughed and spritely jumped his brawn down to the ground to haul their suitcases into the back.

Addie and Lottie climbed up onto the seat and Clay took his driver's place next to Adelaide. "I figured I should see you girls off. How are you going to manage those heavy loads?"

Addie answered because Lottie was eating a doughnut she had pulled from her pocket. "We only have to manage them on and off the trains."

"I'm sure there will be a strong-armed man around to lend a hand to damsels in distress."

Addie didn't find Clay's joviality amusing. "We don't plan on being in distress or looking for a strong-armed man."

Clay craned his neck and addressed Lottie, "How about you, Lottie? Wouldn't you let a strapping young man hoist your suitcase?"

"If I was tired enough, I'd let him hoist me."

Lottie's dry humor gave them all a chuckle.

Clay drove the buggy across the railroad tracks in town and turned left to the handsome, yellow brick station. He offered a hand to each as they left the buggy, then pulled their cases from the back. "I'll wait until you board the train."

"No, Clay," said Addie. "There's sure to be someone who will see us leave and run tattling. No one but you and our parents know we are going. If you wait around, who knows what kind of a tale will be spread around town?"

"I suppose I just have to tip my cap to you lovely ladies as though I've done you a courtesy by giving you a ride."

Lottie gave a wry smile. "I do believe you caught the idea."

He smiled before climbing up into the buggy. "Have a safe journey. Addie you be sure and write."

"I will."

The young women watched him ride away before they picked up their heavy loads and went inside the station. They were fifteen minutes early. The anxious adventurers sat on a bench to await the

103

Norfolk and Western train that would carry them on the first leg of their journey to the West.

Chapter 17

Both Adelaide and Lottie were in awe when the train reached its final destination in Hagerstown at the Western Maryland Train Station. The huge brick two-and-a- half story building with its classical detailing was the grandest piece of architecture they had ever seen.

As the girls stood staring at the massive structure, a gentleman came up behind them. "She's a beauty, isn't she? Only two years old."

His voice startled the two. They turned their heads in unison to see who was speaking. The sallow-faced man looked to be in his forties. He wore a black overcoat, too large for his frail frame, and a gray homburg hat, badly in need of blocking. He paid no attention to Addie and Lottie but kept his eyes on the building and continued his admiration. "Look at those fancy cornices and that porch that wraps around. The three sides of the roof are cantilevered, you know."

Of course neither of them knew exactly what he was talking about.

"Did you build it?" asked Lottie.

The man smiled revealing tobacco-stained teeth. "I used to come every day and watch it go up."

"Don't you work?" asked Adelaide, incredulous that a person could spend every day watching a building being erected.

"Used to, but I can't anymore." he said. "I got bad lungs."

"We're going out to Colorado. I hear the dry air is good for people with bad lungs," offered Lottie.

Adelaide shot her a look of caution.

He offered an appreciative smile. "Neither one of you pretty girls look like you've got bad lungs."

"We haven't," said Addie. "Come on, Lottie. We don't want to miss our train."

"You look like you could spare a couple of dimes," said the stranger.

Before Lottie could answer, Addie remarked, "No we couldn't. Pick up your suitcase, Lottie, we are going into the station."

Lottie did as she was told. They left the man standing there.

"He may have needed money to buy food," Lottie suggested.

"With those stained teeth? If he can afford tobacco, he can afford food."

"He was a nice man and spoke well," Lottie protested.

"If he was a nice man, he wouldn't have asked us for money. Gosh sakes, Lottie. We need every dime we have so don't go feeling sorry for every nice bum we run into."

Inside the huge station, they walked to the ticket counter to buy tickets for Chicago. They each paid their fare and asked directions to the Baltimore and Ohio railroad track that would take them on their next leg of the journey. The train would leave at three-thirty. They had twenty minutes to wait before boarding.

"I'm hungry," said Lottie.

"I've got some gingersnaps. Do you want a couple? They have a dining car on this train. If we eat around six-thirty that will hold us until breakfast."

They sat on a long wooden bench where Adelaide pulled the cookies from a small paper bag in her large pocketbook. They nibbled on the cookies while they watched the people entering and leaving the station.

"The people here in Maryland don't look any different than those in Virginia," observed Lottie.

"I wouldn't think they would. People from the East look like people from the East. Zane Grey is always writing about the long, lean Texans and the wild and wooly men out West. The Western girls he writes about are slender and pretty. Maybe the people out there will look different."

Lottie smiled. "You read too many Western books."

"Probably. If I didn't, maybe we wouldn't be right here where we are."

Lottie smiled. "I guess when we get to where we're going, we'll know if we did the right thing."

"And, if we don't go, we will ask ourselves forever if we should have gone."

Lottie sighed. "You're right. We know we can both go home whenever we need to. Right?"

Addie stood up and picked up her suitcase. "Right."

They walked out to the platform where they saw Baltimore and Ohio written in big white letters on the black rail cars. The conductor told them to leave the suitcases. The bags would go into the baggage car until they reached the end of the line.

The conductor gave them a hand as they stepped up the iron steps to the deck of the passenger car. "Ladies take the seats up front. You will be closer to the dining car and first to leave the train when we reach Chicago," he advised.

Addie and Lottie walked up the aisle of the long rail car. Once in the seat, the two friends found the view was better, and, if anyone smoked, the offensive odor wouldn't be curling into their faces.

Little was said as the young women watched the scenery pass by. The train climbed mountains in West Virginia and crossed the Ohio River into the state of Ohio.

"I smell food," said Lottie.

Addie looked at the watch that had been a gift from Clay Lockwood. "It is five o'clock by my watch. We should wait until six-thirty."

"I can't wait that long. Those gingersnaps only go so far. Let's eat at six. Maybe I can snatch something to eat in case I get hungry before breakfast."

With mild reluctance, Addie agreed. "Don't be obvious if you get a chance to slip something into your pocketbook."

Lottie snickered. "I'll try to be good."

They had to walk through one more passenger car to get to the dining car, which was almost full to capacity. A colored waiter seated them at a table, covered with a white linen cloth, where a lady sat.

She looked up and smiled. "Welcome," she addressed them both. "I prefer to have company rather than to eat by myself. I am Marjorie Hughes from Washington, D.C."

Adelaide made the introductions to the attractive lady wearing a high-necked beige dress and fancy hat to match. The girls could tell she came from a well-to-do family by the expensive jewelry she wore.

She spied the watch Addie wore pinned on her dress. "That's a lovely piece," she said.

"It was a gift," was Addie's reply.

"I'm going to Chicago to meet my husband," Marjorie advised. "He had to on ahead of me for a business meeting. Where are you girls headed?"

"We're going to Colorado," said Addie.

"My goodness, that is definitely in the West. Are you going to Denver?"

"No," Lottie informed. "We're going to Leadville. We hear there are jobs there."

The woman opened her eyes wide. "Jobs?"

Addie attempted to clarify, "We graduated high school in June and decided to go on an adventure."

"I understand that Leadville is a mining town."

"It is," answered Addie. "My father has a friend who wrote that there are opportunities for young women."

The woman shrugged a shoulder. "I'm sure there are all kinds of opportunities for young women out there. You have gone from home with your parents' blessing?"

"Mine were all for it," said Lottie. "Addie's mother was disappointed she didn't go on to school to become a teacher."

The lady wiped her mouth with a linen napkin. "That might have been the wiser choice. It was nice to chat with you girls. I wish you well."

After she left, Lottie turned to Addie. "I don't think she is keen on our going to Leadville."

"Slip that apple into your pocketbook and I'll signal for the bill."

They paid the check and went back to their seats. The porter came by with a blanket and two small pillows. "Making you ladies a bit more comfortable before we reach Chicago. It will be a long night."

Chapter 18

Addie and Lottie spent two nights on the train before reaching the cavernous Chicago station in late afternoon on the third day where they sat on the nearest bench.

"We should ride in one of those Pullman cars. I can't sleep sitting up and my body hurts all over," Lottie complained.

"I told you those kind of tickets cost more. We'll catch up on our sleep when we get to Leadville. Are you hungry? The next train doesn't leave for two hours."

Lottie yawned. "I'd rather sleep."

"Come on," encouraged Adelaide. "You'll feel better after we get something to eat."

"Why don't I just sit here on this bench, and you go find food and bring it back to me?"

"Because we need to stretch our legs after being cramped up on the train," Addie answered, with annoyance in her voice.

"Don't get miffed. I've got my second wind. With luck, I can make it to a restaurant."

They walked out of Chicago's huge, brick Grand Central Station that sported a tower. The girls stopped to look up and wondered, if one climbed to the top of that tower could one see Lake Michigan?

A few doors away was a café. Most of the tables were full of diners. A lady sat by herself and motioned the two young women to sit with her. They gladly took seats at the small table.

"If you have a train to catch, you should order as soon as the waiter stops by. As you can see, they are busy. I'd order the special of the day if I were you."

"What is that?" asked Lottie.

The woman pointed to her plate. "Meatloaf, gravy, carrots, and mashed potatoes."

Addie wasn't sure she cared for the woman's forward manner, but she had offered them a place to sit so she withheld judgement. "That should fill us up," she said to Lottie.

The woman wore a long black dress and a large black hat with a spray of feathers attached to the side. "Where are you girls headed?"

"Colorado," answered Adelaide.

The waiter came by and took their order after he poured each a glass of water.

The woman did not look up from the plate of food she was eating. "Denver?"

"No, Leadville," said Lottie.

She looked up then and pointed her fork. With a deep, husky voice, she warned, "You be on your toes. Lots of ruffians out there."

"Where are you going?" asked Lottie.

The woman wiped her mouth with a cloth napkin and pushed her plate aside. "I'm going to Denver to a suffragette rally. Susan B. Anthony and Carrie Chapman Catt will be speakers."

The girls must have looked bewildered because she leaned across the table and said, "Don't tell me you young ladies don't know about the Suffragette Movement!"

"We read about it in school," Addie informed.

"And, once there was a parade in town where the suffragette women dressed in their white uniforms and rode horses," added Lottie.

"Hah!" exclaimed the woman.

Addie and Lottie were both grateful for the waiter bringing their food at that point. They began eating in earnest.

Although she had finished her dinner, the woman remained seated. "It is young ladies like you who need to get behind this movement. Don't you care if you get the right to vote? Do you think it is right that men run everything?"

They didn't care either way, but they were not about to tell this lady of their ambivalence to the cause.

For one hour they tolerated the woman's lecture on the whole struggle and the noteworthy people who were leading the charge. According to the lecturer, she would meet with Margaret Brown, a millionaire from Denver who stood solidly behind the suffragettes

As the mention of Margaret Brown did not bring a comment from the girls, the suffragette proceeded to tell them. "Now don't tell me you young women have never heard of "the Unsinkable

Molly Brown" who survived the tragedy of the Titanic last year."

Addie gave a hurried reply. "We read about it in the newspaper."

She checked the watch Clay had given her. "My goodness, Lottie, we have to hurry. The train leaves in twenty minutes."

"What train are you taking?" asked the lady.

"We're taking the Chicago, Burlington and Quincy to Denver," Addie answered in a confident manner.

The woman brightened. "A coincidence. I will be on the same train. I have a private compartment. You girls are welcome to share it with me."

Addie discreetly kicked Lottie before she could speak. "Thank you. That's a kind offer, but we have a space reserved."

At that, Lottie turned and sent a disgusted look to her not so truthful friend.

The three walked together back to the grand Chicago station. Dusk was setting in and there was a light mist in the air before they parted ways when they boarded the train.

Addie and Lottie hurried to get one of the front seats in the coach. There didn't seem to be anything different about this train than the last two they were on. It was just as loud, grungy and smoky as the others.

After they settled into their seats, Lottie asked, "Why didn't you take that woman up on her offer? Maybe we could get some decent rest. I'd like to see what a private compartment looks like."

"And listen to that woman drone on and on about women getting the vote? No thank you. I'd rather be cramped up here than to have to listen to her all the way to Denver."

"When are we supposed to get there?"

"Day after tomorrow. If it will make you feel better, I slipped a couple of rolls into a bag in my purse."

"Ooh, I feel better all ready," came Lottie's sarcastic reply. "We can eat them in this lovely reserved space when we're wide-eyed at two o'clock in the morning."

"You'll be fine when we reach Denver. We can get a room for the night because the train to Leadville doesn't leave until the next morning."

Lottie came to attention. "You never told me that. What else haven't you told me? It's good your uncle gave you that extra money. I think we're going to need it."

Sometimes Lottie Bell Foster could be irksome and this was one of those times. "Curl up and get some sleep, Lottie."

Chapter 19

"Denver, ten minutes ahead," announced the conductor causing Addie and Lottie to sit up straight.

"Thank goodness," said Adelaide. "I've seen enough corn fields, wheat fields and flat land out of these smoky windows to last me for the next ten years."

Lottie stretched her arms and rubbed her tired eyes. "Every joint and bone in my body aches, I hope we find a decent place to sleep tonight."

"I asked the conductor if he knew of a nearby hotel. He said The Oxford Hotel on 17th street. It is more expensive but safe and within walking distance."

"As long as I can sleep in a bed, it will be worth extra money."

Addie smiled at her friend. "I'll use some of the money Uncle Frank gave me."

Lottie looked skeptical. "I thought you were going to reserve that for my return ticket home if I needed it."

"I'll replace it once I get a job."

"You mean if you get a job."

The train jerked to a halt. The two young women picked up their tote bags and pocketbooks and made ready to depart the train at the busy Denver Union Station. The conductor had their suitcases ready on the platform when they stepped off.

Addie and Lottie walked past the Mountain States Telephone and Telegraph counter where a well-dressed gentleman was talking to the clerk. No one paid any attention to the two plain young women from Virginia gaping at the ornate cornices and elegant chandeliers adorning the attractive depot.

Lottie whispered to Addie," Look at that line of telephone booths. Can you imagine?"

They stopped to take them in. Each booth was decorated in molded tin and sported a number above the door. Behind the line of small compartments sat an operator wearing a headset. In front of her was a big board where she busily plugged and unplugged wires. Lights came on the board when she plugged in a wire and off when she removed it.

They made their way out of the two-story stone building and turned to look back. A large clock tower stood sentinel next to arched windows. The second floor of the building had decorative ironwork that resembled a picket fence. Stone cornices gave the building a feeling of grandeur.

They walked under a tall arch with the word "Mizpah" written on it.

"I wonder what that means?" said Lottie.

"That comes from the bible."

"How do you know?"

"I read about it. It means something like looking down from a high place."

117

"Do you mean like God looking down from heaven or someone looking down from the top of one of those Rocky Mountains?"

Addie was trying to get her bearings. "I don't know, Lottie. I don't think they had the Rocky Mountains in the book of Genesis. We need to find 17th Street."

The streets were busy with buggies, wagons and pedestrians. Unfazed by her friend's mild reproof, Lottie said, "This sign says 16th Street. Seems to me we need to walk a block that way."

While they were debating, a tall, lean, young man wearing a cowboy hat, neckerchief, plaid shirt and well-worn pants approached.

"You young ladies look like you can use a hand. Those cases look mighty heavy."

"We can manage," was Addie's curt reply.

"How much will it cost for you to carry them to The Oxford Hotel?" asked Lottie.

"Shucks, ma'am. That ain't gonna' cost you a penny. Caleb Dunn at yer service." He touched the brim of his large hat. "I'd be proud to carry them fer you."

"Do you know where The Oxford hotel is?" asked Adelaide.

"One of the classiest hotels in Denver. I shur do." He hoisted the two suitcases, one in each strong hand. "Follow me," he ordered.

Addie and Lottie looked at each other and shrugged their shoulders. They carried a tote in one hand and a large pocketbook in the other as they dutifully followed the amiable cowboy.

They crossed a cobblestone street and waited for a wagon that had The Seattle Creamery Company written on its side. Streetcars made their way over the tramways.

As a way of making conversation, Addie asked, "Do you live here?"

"I'm from Oklahoma. I ben' up here fer about six months. Right now I'm workin' fer a company that supplies equipment to the miners in Leadville. I go lookin' fer a strike on the weekends. There's still gotta' be a lot of ore in those mountains."

"Leadville!" exclaimed Lottie. "That's where we're headed."

Addie gave her a cautious look.

He turned his head with a look of surprise. "It's kind of a wild place fer girls like you," he said.

"My father's friend wrote a letter that there are a lot of jobs there," offered Addie as a way of explanation.

"Where are you all from?" he asked.

"A small town in Virginia," Addie answered before Lottie could open her mouth.

He stopped in front of a brick five-story building. "I shur hope you know what yer doin'. This is the Oxford."

"We should give you something for your trouble," said Addie.

"No, ma'am. I wish you ladies luck," he said and touched the brim of his hat before he turned and loped down the street.

"He was right nice," Lottie surmised as she watched him go.

A door attendant held the door as they walked into the opulent lobby decorated with oak and leather furniture, silver chandeliers and frescoed walls. Western artwork was in abundance.

Lottie and Addie knew they were out of their league the minute they entered. Well-dressed travelers discreetly eyed the young women as they made their way to the counter.

Adelaide took charge. "We would like a room for tonight."

The clerk looked at them. "There are less expensive hotels," he said.

Adelaide felt her face redden. "Of course there are. We would like a room here."

The clerk cleared his throat. He reached behind him and took a key from the wall. "We have a room on the fourth floor for five dollars."

"Thank you." Addie fished around in her pocketbook and took a five-dollar bill from a small clasped case. She unfolded the bill and smoothed it out as she handed it to the clerk.

He turned the ledger toward them so they could each write her name. "I'll get someone to carry your bags," he said.

"That isn't necessary," Addie answered.

"The elevator is to your left at the end of the lobby."

They picked up their suitcases with the nonchalance of those who rode elevators on a daily basis and headed in the direction in which the clerk pointed.

Lottie leaned over to Addie and whispered, "Addie, we don't know anything about elevators."

"Let's pretend we do. There are people waiting there; we'll just follow what they do."

They waited with a small group and jumped when the elevator landed with a loud clank. To their relief there was an attendant at the control.

"Good afternoon, everyone. Welcome to the Oxford Hotel. The elevator stops at every floor. Who could ask for more?" He laughed at his own attempt at humor, which did nothing to ease the girls' apprehension. The two friends left the elevator when it reached the fourth floor and followed arrows on the wall that pointed to room numbers.

Addie turned the key in the lock and pushed the door open with her shoulder. They almost swooned when they entered. The mahogany bed with curves in the wooden headboard stood high off the floor. A small stepstool was tucked underneath to be pulled out for crawling onto the bed.

"Oh, Addie. Isn't this wonderful? Look, there's a writing desk with a pen and paper." Lottie hurried to the desk and pulled a chain on a small gold lamp. "Electric lights! And look at those lovely red velvet drapes." Lottie ran to the drapes and pulled them apart. "Addie we can see the mountains! How majestic they look."

Addie was exploring the bathroom. "Lottie, we've got a claw foot tub and a separate water closet! The faucets look like they're made of gold."

Lottie came to join her friend. "Addie, I think we've died and gone to heaven."

They removed their ankle-length boots and cotton stockings to feel the luxury of the patterned carpet under their bare feet.

They danced around and fell into two upholstered chairs. "I wonder if Uncle Frank would approve of how I'm spending the money he gave me," mused Adelaide.

"I doubt it. It's also the money you're supposed to save for my trip back home," advised Lottie as she climbed up onto the bed.

"Are you sorry?"

"Not a bit. I wish I could lay in this bed for a week"

"I wish you could too. Let's put on our Sunday dresses and go find something to eat. Maybe we'll look like we belong in this hotel."

"Let's," agreed Lottie.

They scrubbed their faces, fixed their hair and put on their best dresses. Lottie wore her gold locket and Addie pinned on the watch that Clay Lockwood had given her.

They felt like proper ladies as they took the elevator to the lobby.

As they walked toward the front door, they heard a voice call, "Yoo-hoo, girls."

They turned to see the middle-aged suffragette lady they had met on the train.

Addie groaned.

"How fortunate to meet up with you young ladies once again. Are you on your way to dinner?"

What could they say but yes?

"There is a charming little café a couple doors down. I would enjoy treating you both to a meal."

"That's kind of you, but we…"

"We would be delighted," Lottie interrupted.

The trio went to the small and crowded café where they spent one hour listening to the lady lead the charge on the Suffragette Movement. They didn't have to say a word. They offered either a smile or nod all through their dinner of steak and potatoes. The waiter offered pie for dessert.

Addie saw Lottie's eyes light up, but she had enough of the ongoing lecture. "We couldn't eat another bite," she said.

Lottie was not to be thwarted. "Speak for yourself, Adelaide." Lottie smiled at their benefactor. "I would love to have a piece of pie and hear more about the suffragettes."

Back in their room at the hotel Addie was miffed. "I hope you enjoyed that pie. The woman bores me to death."

"She was nice enough to buy our dinners. You could afford to be cordial."

"We could have found a cheaper place to eat."

"I suppose we could have bought a package of Fig Newtons," replied Lottie. "I, for one, savored the steak and potatoes."

Addie relaxed. "It was nice of her to buy us a meal. Maybe I'm just worn out."

"Let's take a warm bath and crawl into this comfortable bed. What time does our train to Leadville leave?"

"Nine-fifteen."

"Good. We won't have to get out of bed until eight-fifteen."

"That won't give time for breakfast."

"I noticed a basket of fruit on the counter that reads: For Our Guests. I slipped a couple of apples and two oranges into my pocketbook."

"You don't miss much, Lottie."

She smiled. "Not when it comes to food."

Chapter 20

Addie awoke with a start. "What's that noise?"

Lottie never moved from her curled up position in the comfortable ed. "It sounds like steam hissing through the radiators like they did in school," was her drowsy reply.

Addie sat up on the edge of the bed and stretched her arms above her head. "Can you imagine waking up in a warm room? Waking up without greasy food smells or noise of rattling dishes or a baby crying? Aren't we lucky, Lottie? I'm so glad you decided to come with me. To tell you the truth, I wasn't brave enough to come by myself."

Lottie turned over on her back. "If you're going to talk, I suppose I have to wake up. What time is it?"

Addie checked her watch, which she had placed on a bedside table. "Seven-thirty."

Mildly irritated, Lottie said, "I could have slept for another forty-five minutes."

"This will give us time to have breakfast," said Addie, hoping that would soothe Lottie's annoyance at being awakened sooner than she wanted.

The suggestion seemed to please her friend. "Breakfast sounds good. We can eat in that café we ate in last evening. Maybe we won't have to eat again until we get to Leadville. The train food is expensive. I'm beginning to get antsy about spending money." It was unlike Lottie to be concerned.

Addie was also, but she was not to let Lottie know. "This will be our last train ticket to buy. We won't stay in a fancy hotel like this again. Don't you think it was worth extra money?"

Lottie sat up. "Yes, it was worth it. I slept well. No more aches and pains from those tortuous train rides. If we go back home, Addie, I'm going to save enough money for one of those private compartments. Someday I'll bet they'll be carting travelers around in airplanes."

"Let's not think about going home. We haven't even got to Leadville yet."

Even the bathroom was toasty warm as the girls washed up and combed their hair.

After Addie donned the mustard colored dress, one more time, she piled her hair up under the brown straw hat she bought at Catherine Ramsburg's shop in Berryville.

Lottie opened the long red velvet drapes. "I just want one more view of those beautiful mountains to sink into my memory. Addie, Denver is so alive I'm not sure I could ever go back and live in Berryville."

"What about Sam? Are you truly over him? You said all you wanted to do was to marry him and settle down."

Lottie stood gazing out the window. "That was before this trip opened my eyes. My parents were right. It is good to get out and see more of the world."

Addie stood behind her friend looking out at the Rockies. "I wish Momma saw it that way. I know she is still hurt that I didn't go to the normal school."

"She'll get over it. I'm packed. Are you ready?"

"I am."

Out the door they went, pleased that they didn't even have to make the bed. They took the key to the clerk at the counter after riding the elevator down.

Dressed in their ugly dresses and plain coats they didn't look like they belonged in this fancy hotel. They didn't care. The two country girls from Virginia had learned to use an elevator, luxuriated in a room beyond their dreams, and paid their five dollars the same as other guests. It mattered not how they were dressed. In this place where those going east passed those going west, they felt a whole head taller as they walked out onto the cobbled stones of 17th Street and breathed in clear mountain air.

Addie was relieved the café was less crowded than the evening before and without any sign of the suffragette woman. She could eat her breakfast without having to listen to the woman's spiel about voting rights. Addie had seen pictures of those women. They looked old and stern. With the uncertainty of what they would find in Leadville on her mind, she didn't have time to worry about women voting.

127

There was a table with two chairs setting near a window at the back of the café with enough room to put their suitcases and tote bags without being in the way of others.

The waiter in a bib apron brought a menu to the table. "Special this morning is two scrambled eggs, bacon, sausage, biscuits with gravy and fried potatoes for one dollar and a quarter. That includes coffee."

"That's what we'll have," said Lottie without asking Addie. "We would like the gravy on the side."

"Both want coffee?" he asked.

"They nodded their heads.

"Comin' right up."

"Lottie that's a lot of food. I couldn't possibly eat that much."

"If we get the gravy on the side we can put the sausage and bacon in the biscuits and have them for lunch on the train."

"Good thinking," said Addie. This plan gave Lottie a whole new dimension in Addie's eyes. Maybe she had been remiss in not crediting Lottie with solid thoughts. But then, it was difficult to best Lottie when it came to food.

Back at Denver Union Station, Addie asked directions to the Denver & Rio Grande line. Of course a porter wanted to carry their bags and of course they refused. Addie had spent some of the extra money Uncle Frank had given her and twenty dollars on train tickets. She had thirty dollars left.

She hoped it would be enough to get her through to a first paycheck.

Lottie told her that she had twenty-five dollars. Between them Addie figured they had enough money to rent a room and eat even if they didn't get a job right away. She hoped so.

The conductor came by and punched a hole in their tickets. "Leavin' right on time. I see you young ladies are goin' all the way to Leadville. You got relatives out there?"

"No, sir," answered Addie. "My father has a friend who said there are lots of opportunities there."

"Is this friend of your father's meetin' you at the train?"

It wasn't any of his business, but Adelaide remained polite. "We will be going to a rooming house he mentioned."

Lottie looked at her wide-eyed.

"That's good," said the conductor. "Leadville isn't a place for young girls on their own."

After he continued down the aisle, Lottie leaned toward Addie. "You told another fib. We don't know of any rooming house, and you don't even know that man who wrote to your father. That isn't like you."

"It wasn't the conductor's business. We're free to travel wherever we want."

"He was only being helpful. I'm beginning to get nervous about going to this place. Every person we've talked to has discouraged us." The look on her pleasingly plump face told of her concern.

In truth, Addie was beginning to have second thoughts but she wouldn't let on to Lottie. This trip had all been her doing. She would see it through. She would also see that Lottie got back to Virginia if she had to.

"End of the line. All out for Leadville," shouted the conductor. "Good luck to you girls."

Excitement and anticipation gripped Adelaide Mae Richards and Lottie Bell Foster as they prepared to depart for their long-awaited destination.

They stepped onto the wooden platform of the train depot and viewed their surroundings. High in the mountains of Leadville, Colorado, two-thousand miles from their bucolic Virginia, smiles faded at the sights that greeted them. The once beautiful mountains were scarred by shacks, downed timber, and mines. Ore smelters belched smoke. Poorly dressed men eyed them with curiosity, and the thin mountain air smelled of the grime of mining. They stood speechless. Addie managed to say, "Oh Lottie! Have I made a big mistake for both of us?"

Chapter 21

Laura Richards was up early. If she had a good night's sleep since Adelaide left over two weeks ago, she couldn't recall. She thought she had made her peace with her daughter, but it still hurt that Addie had not gone along with her wishes to go to the normal school. She would make a good teacher, thought Laura. One day Addie will be sorry; she knew it.

John Richards came into the kitchen. "You're up early. Worried about Addie?"

"I think she should have written by now. It's inconsiderate of her not to let us know where she is or if all is going well."

"She'll do fine. Just goin' about her business and not thinkin' about the rest of us. Headstrong in her ways, like her mother," he teased as he kissed his wife on the cheek. He placed his work-worn hands on her shoulders. "She and Lottie will use their heads. Have you talked to Lottie's mother?"

Laura nodded. "She hasn't had any word either."

"I'm sure they're busy gettin' settled. Give it another week. I'll be back for breakfast." He took his hat off a peg near the door and left the house.

Laura went out and sat in a rocker on the porch. She didn't need to start breakfast yet. The children were still asleep and the quiet of the early morning allowed her mind to wander.

She hadn't seen Alex Lockwood since that day at the stream when he encouraged her to let Addie go. Had he set up a law office in Berryville? She had told him to keep his distance and he had. Why did he cloud her thoughts? Soon she would turn thirty-five years old. She was a wife and mother of four children. Why did her mind conjure up thoughts of Alex Lockwood? Because, if she were truthful with herself, she hated losing her youth. She wanted to run up to the big house, watch as Alex saddled their horses and ride off into the fields as they had done so long ago. Laura shook her head to get rid of the vision. Dwelling on what had been wouldn't change a thing, and she knew it.

. With a big sigh, the tired woman rose from the chair and went back into the kitchen to start on the chores of the day.

Even though Addie had not done her will, leaving Berryville got her away from Clayton Lockwood. If something good had to come out of something bad that was it. That was enough to ease Laura's mind that her daughter would not suffer over a lost love as she had.

**

That same morning, Addie Richards and Lottie Foster were sound asleep in a bed in the Delaware Hotel on 6th and Harrison Streets in Leadville. It was not as grand as the Oxford Hotel in Denver, but it had steam heat, hot and cold running water and gas lights. There was a bathroom down the hall that was shared by other guests. The young women decided not to take a bath. The less time they had to spend in the malodorous shared bathroom the better.

Although the first floor of the hotel consisted of store fronts and they had to walk up a flight of stairs, Addie and Lottie chose the Delaware for two reasons. With its mansard roof, it looked much like the Berryville Hotel, and it was cheaper than the Clarendon or Windsor. The ticket master at the depot had suggested the three.

Lottie awoke first and poked Adelaide. "Do you think we should look for a job first or find a place to stay?"

"Did you have to wake me up to ask that?" Addie rubbed the sleep from her pretty hazel eyes. "I noticed a café a couple of doors away. Maybe we can have breakfast there and ask someone where there are boarding places. Are you sorry you came, Lottie?"

"Not yet, but I'm getting close. If I wasn't so tired yesterday, I think I would have broken down in tears after our bubble burst at the sights in this place."

"We have to give it a chance. Let's hurry and get dressed."

They both wore white waists and different colored ankle length skirts thinking they would look more hirable to prospective employers. Addie's skirt was a navy blue plaid. She opted for the navy cloche hat. Lottie's skirt was tan.

"I should wear that brown straw hat of yours, Addie. It would look good with my skirt."

"Go ahead. Miss Ramsburg knew what she was doing when she sold me these hats. In truth, she gave me the brown as a present for doing so well in school."

Lottie placed the hat over her puffed sandy colored hair. "Lucky you. How do I look?"

"You look good. I think you have lost some weight since we left home."

"Why wouldn't I with all that walking and lugging? I can't afford to lose weight or my clothes won't fit."

Addie smiled.

They hadn't had a good look at the town but they had passed some shops and stores on the way that looked like places to apply for jobs.

"I hope this is the last time I have to haul this suitcase around," complained Lottie. "It gets heavier every time I pick it up."

"Food will give you more energy," assured Adelaide as she pulled the room key from her pocket to leave at the desk.

Lottie sighed. "I doubt it." "I hope that café has doughnuts. Let's drag ourselves out to see what the world has in store for us today."

Chapter 22

Those in the small eating place looked up when the two young women entered. Most of those were men of different ages, sizes and dress. Undaunted by the ogling and mild commotion they caused, Addie and Lottie toted their suitcases to a small table and placed the cases on the wood floor next to their chairs.

Before a waiter came to wait on them, a young man dressed in cowboy attire rose from his chair to come by their spot.

"I declare. The two ladies from Virginia who I met in Denver." He doffed his high hat and placed it back on his head.

While Addie struggled to remember his name, Lottie burst forth with, "Why, Mr. Dunn. This is a surprise."

"Do you mind if I pull up a chair. I'll grab my cup of coffee."

He didn't wait for an answer.

"Lottie we need to be careful. We don't know anything about him."

"Addie. He was nice and carried our bags for us. The least we can do is allow him to join us for breakfast."

Addie shook her head. "I'm beginning to think you find all men nice."

The male waiter took their order: flapjacks, scrambled eggs and coffee.

"Do you have doughnuts?" Lottie asked.

The waiter thumbed in the direction of the counter where fried doughnuts sat in a small display case.

"I'll take two."

Caleb Dunn arrived with cup in hand and swung his long leg over the café chair. "When did you ladies get in?"

"Last evening," advised Lottie. "We stayed at the Delaware Hotel."

"What are your plans now?"

"We need to find a rooming house."

Addie looked at her friend under hooded eyes with a look that said Lottie was being too informative.

"You gals want to stay away from the 2nd Street area. Gambling and bawdy houses down there."

"Where do you suggest, Mr. Dunn?" asked an interested Addie.

"You gals call me Caleb."

"I'm Lottie and this is Addie."

There was another dark look from Adelaide.

"Ol' Miz' Tygert has a boarder. If she's got a room that would be the place."

"Is it expensive?" asked Lottie, who was beginning to be concerned about finances just in case she wanted a ticket home.

"No more'n any other respectable place around here. I'd be pleased to show you ladies the way."

"Aren't you supposed to be working or something?" asked Addie, suspicious of the free time Caleb seemed to have.

"Funny thing is that I'm startin' a new job on Monday. Gonna' be dumpin' ore into railroad cars. Pay's better."

"I thought you said you came to Leadville to look for gold," said Lottie.

"I did, but my pardner backed out sayin' he thought it was foolhardy. He went on back to Oklahoma to punch cows."

The waiter brought their meals and two hungry young women ate in earnest.

Adelaide was eager to get on with the next order of business. "Where does this Mrs. Tygert live? Is she alone or does she have a husband?"

Caleb drained the coffee in his cup before he answered. "She's a widow. Husband's been dead for a couple years. She takes in boarders to make ends meet."

"You seem to be familiar with her," said Addie.

"I happened to be walkin' by her place while she was tryin' to coax her cat down from a tree. I was tall enough to reach up and pull him down. Ornery thing almost bit me. Anyways, we got to talkin'. She a fine lady."

The girls finished their breakfast and Caleb picked up the tab.

137

"Oh, no," said Adelaide. "That wouldn't be right for you to pay for our meals."

Lottie was quick to speak. "That is nice of you, Caleb. Adelaide and I are most appreciative. And, if you have time, it would be helpful to show us to Mrs. Tygert's house."

Caleb went to pay the check.

"Lottie, what's got into you?"

"We're saving money and he'll carry our suitcases. Besides, I think he is right nice."

"You would," said a disgusted Adelaide.

"You gals ready?" asked a cheerful Caleb Dunn. "Let me hoist them cases you got crammed full." He grinned from ear to ear as he picked one up in each hand and stretched his arms above his head. "Light as a feather." Much to Adelaide's embarrassment, the patrons snickered as they watched the trio leave.

Adelaide leaned toward Lottie. "He's a showoff," she whispered.

Lottie chuckled. "That doesn't bother me a bit. I think he's cute."

Chapter 23

The three were a curiosity as they walked up the main street of Leadville on the board sidewalk.

"This is Harrison Street. Pretty much it's where everything's at," said Caleb acting as a tour guide.

"Is this the better side of town," asked Adelaide as they walked along.

"Might say that. The town's got everythin' people need from a telephone and telegraph office to an opera house."

"We have that in Berryville." advised Lottie.

Addie didn't want her friend to think too much about home. "But Lottie, our Blue Ridge Mountains can't compare to the high peaks of these Rocky Mountains. They climb to the sky."

"It feels like this whole place touches the sky. I'm beginning to miss the trees and the hills of Virginia," answered Lottie.

Caleb still carried the suitcases as though they were light weight. "Ladies, we turn left at the next corner and it's a couple of houses down."

They followed his directions noting the post office on a corner. "We have to write to our parents, Lottie. They are probably concerned about us."

"Let's find a place to stay before we worry about that."

Caleb stopped in front of a modest Victorian house.

Addie opened the gate of a white picket fence. They went up five wooden steps onto a covered porch where two empty rocking chairs sat side by side. Caleb set the suitcases down and knocked on the door. Through the leaded glass pane they could see a figure coming down a narrow hall.

A wisp of a lady with gray hair pulled back into a bun opened the door. It took her a few seconds before she recognized Caleb. "Why, Mr. Dunn, how nice to see you." She looked from Addie to Lottie. "And, who are these two lovely young ladies?"

He tipped the brim of his hat in acknowledgement. "Miz' Tygert, meet Miz' Addie and Miz' Lottie. They just came all the way from Virginia. I told them you might have a room to let."

"Please come in," she invited as she backed away and opened the door wide.

They entered onto a flat landing at the foot of a staircase. A step down to the right was the parlor.

The lady of the house led the way. "Come, sit."

The low-ceilinged room was comfortable with two tapestry covered chairs setting each side of a small fireplace with an ornate mahogany couch covered in maroon velvet facing all three. A low table sat in front of the couch. A rocking chair and easy chair sat in corners of the rom.

Addie and Lottie opted for the tapestry chairs, Caleb sat on the bottom step of the staircase.

"Mr. Dunn, won't you come and join us?"

"No thank you, ma'am. My boots have collected dirt from the streets. I'm mighty fine right here."

"As you wish. Now, girls we need a proper introduction. My name is Anna Tygert."

"I'm Adelaide Richards and this is my best friend, Lottie Foster."

"And, you are from Virginia. The "Old Dominion" I believe they call it."

"Yes, ma'am. We live in the very northern part."

"Near Washington, D.C.?" she asked.

"Oh no. We live in a town about seventy miles from there. The nearest city is called Winchester."

"I've heard of that."

The young women looked at each other in amazement.

"Mr. Tygert was quite the scholar of the Civil War. He had a map of where all the battles were fought. It seemed Virginia had more than its share. He always said, 'One day we're going to take a trip back there'. Of course, we never did before Mr. Tygert passed away." There was a look of sadness in her face as she recalled his words.

Lottie was remorseful. "Mrs. Tygert, I'm sorry you lost your husband, and I'm sorry you never got to take the trip."

141

"Don't feel bad, dear. Mr. Tygert was the one who talked about going, not I. I'm very happy tucked away here in the mountains. Now, tell me why you have come."

Adelaide leaned forward in her chair. "Lottie and I graduated from high school this year and we wanted to have an adventure before we settled down. A friend of my father's wrote that there are many opportunities out here so we came to find ours."

"Two young girls traveling alone? Did your parents approve?"

"Mine did but Addie's didn't," Lottie informed.

Adelaide was quick to explain. "My mother had her heart set on me becoming a teacher. I can always go to school later."

Anna Tygert sat for a moment seeming to let this information settle in her mind. "That must have been a disappointment for your mother, but I can understand you young girls. There are many more opportunities for women than when I was your age. Did you want to be a teacher, Adelaide?"

"I will be honest and tell you that it was my mother's dream, not mine."

"Then you are wise to take time in making a decision. My boarder teaches at the Leadville High School up on 9th Street. I sometimes suspect that she would rather have taken a different path."

Adelaide was to the point. "Mrs. Tygert, we need to rent a room. Do you have one available?"

The lady hesitated before she spoke. "I only have two rooms to let and, as I told you, I have a tenant in one. If you girls want to share a room I could let you rent the other. It's not a big room but it will allow two twin beds and a small dresser for each."

"May we see it?" asked Addie.

"Of course. Follow me up the stairs."

Caleb rose from the step to allow them to pass.

"If the girls are interested, Mr. Dunn, we may need your muscle to change a few things around." She reached up and patted his shoulder as she passed.

The staircase split at the top. Two steps up to the left was Mrs. Tygert's room, straight ahead was the bathroom and to the right was the teacher's room. The vacant room was a few steps farther down a short hallway overlooking the staircase.

Anna Tygert stood in the hall outside the room. "You girls go right in."

They squeezed past her. The landlady was right. There was just enough room for two beds and two small dressers, although there was only one bed and dresser occupying the room as they looked it over. The ceiling slanted on each side and peaked at the top where a window sat inside a dormer. It was a cozy room with flowered wall paper on the walls. A window seat was beneath the window.

Lottie ran over and knelt on the flowered cushion seat. "Look, Addie. We can see the mountains from here."

143

Addie was reticent. This room wasn't much bigger than her loft bedroom in the tenant house. Their shoes could go under the beds, but where would they put their suitcases?

As if sensing her reluctance, Anna Tygert said from the doorway, "There is extra storage space over here."

Addie went to see where she was talking about. A short door opened into space under the eaves. She stooped over and entered. It could be utilized.

"How much do you charge?" Addie asked.

"I charge three dollars and fifty cents a room per week. That includes breakfast and dinner. You will be responsible for your laundry and cleaning your room. Because you will be sharing the room I will have to charge five dollars a week. Does that sound fair?"

"Yes," agreed Adelaide. "Will we have to sign a paper that says we will rent for a number of weeks?"

"Goodness no, dear. You girls are free to look for other lodging as you please."

Did this liberal outlook mean they weren't going to find anything better or was Mrs. Tygert a sincerely good person? Either way it was a roof over their heads.

Addie snapped up the offer. "We will take it."

Lottie came out of the room as they were talking.

"We will pay five dollars a week and that includes breakfast and dinner."

Lottie shrugged a shoulder. If it was okay with Addie, it was okay with her. She nodded her acceptance.

This pleased Anna Tygert. She clapped her hands together. "How grand. We will need to get Mr. Dunn to haul up the bed and the dresser. They are in the shed out back."

The band of four went out the back door of the house to where the shed sat a few feet away.

Caleb opened the door. The shed was packed to the ceiling. "Goodness me," uttered Mrs. Tygert. "I guess we will have to dig for them," which meant Addie, Lottie, and Caleb while Mrs. Tygert supervised the removal and replacement of all items.

The bed and dresser needed cleaning but they were attractive cherry with bone handles on the two drawer dresser. The mattress had some minor holes from mice but, otherwise, it was in good shape. Lottie and Addie used a broom to bang out the dust in the mattress and any errant mouse who might be living in it while Caleb toted the bed and dresser to their room. He set them up to allow each girl as much space as possible before he climbed over the foot of the bed to exit the room.

With directions from Addie, he hauled the mattress up the staircase and placed it on the bed slats.

"It smells like mothballs," he commented.

145

"Mothballs are supposed to keep the mice and moths away," Addie answered.

"Can't say as it worked."

"It worked well enough."

"I'm not sleeping on that mattress," informed Lottie.

"You won't have to. I don't mind one bit. There wasn't much dust in it, and the mattress protector and sheet are clean so they'll act as a buffer. Caleb thank you so much for all the help you have given us."

"I'm pleased you two are in a safe place. I'll drop by next week to see how you're gettin' along."

Anna Tygert met him at the bottom of the stairs. "Won't you stay for dinner, Mr. Dunn?"

"Thank you ma'am, no. I'm always glad to lend a hand. I told the girls I'd check in next week to see how things are goin' for them."

"I believe that is a wise idea."

He agreed. "It can be a rough town for young ladies who don't know these parts."

"How true. I'm sure the girls are famished. I have dinner ready for them. Good bye, Mr. Dunn, and thank you for bringing the young ladies."

Addie had opened the one window in their room to let the cool air seep in to rid the smell of mothballs.

They had unpacked their suitcases and found places for their belongings. What pleased them most was the discovery that they could hang their dresses in the space under the eaves.

They sat on the edge of their beds facing each other with their knees almost touching.

"What do you think, Lottie?"

She looked around the room before she answered, "Well, let me see. We are sharing a room that is smaller than my old room at home. We had to pay out another five dollars from what little money we have left. We don't have jobs, and I am starved. Other than those minor problems, we seem to be doing just great."

A bell tinkled followed by the sing-song voice of Anna Tygert. "Girls. Soup's on,"

"Oh boy, soup," said Lottie. "I can hardly wait."

Chapter 24

Addie and Lottie were up at six o'clock. The window had been left open so the room was cool that late September morning.

Addie struggled between the beds to close the window. She couldn't help but gaze at the snow-capped mountain peaks. "Waking up to this view puts all of our cares behind us." She turned to Lottie who was sitting up and ruffling her hair.

Lottie sniffed the air. "The smell of mothballs is almost gone. We might have done ourselves in if we hadn't left the window open. You didn't find any unwanted visitors parading around, did you?"

"If you are referring to mice, no. The mattress was more than comfortable."

"I wish I could say the same for this one. It's as hard as a rock."

"If you hadn't been so picky you could have had this one."

Lottie yawned and sat on the edge of her bed. "You'll have to step over me unless you want to walk on the bed."

"Don't move. I need to get my waist and skirt from the closet."

"Closet? You mean the eaves. Our skirts are almost doubled at the bottom. I don't plan on ironing mine."

Addie stepped over Lottie's knees. "We didn't ask about an iron or where the washtubs are for laundering."

"Maybe they're in the shed. Everything else seemed to be in there."

Addie went to retrieve her clothing and was quick to duck back into the bedroom. "Oh, these clothes are cold. Do you want to go into the bathroom before I do?"

"You go first. Maybe the school teacher is in there. I wonder what she's like."

Addie was changing from her long nightgown. "I had hoped to meet her at dinner last evening. Seeing that dinner is part of the rent, I'm surprised she wasn't there."

"It could be that one of the student's parents invited her to their house. They used to do that in Berryville so their kid would get a better grade."

Addie looked at her friend. "Why, Lottie Bell Foster! That isn't true."

"Think about it, Addie. That Smith kid was as dumb as they come but he always passed. I'm sure the fruit and vegetables he brought the teacher did a lot to bring his grades up to a D."

Addie cast a wry look. "I'll hurry. I don't know what time Mrs. Tygert has breakfast."

Lottie stood, scratched her stomach and stretched before she headed for the hideaway. She, too, would wear a skirt and blouse. Today was the big day to find a position. Addie's looks might get her a job but Lottie knew she had to depend on her skills. A thought crossed her mind that it might help if she shed a few pounds.

At six forty-five they heard a loud clang, clang, clang.

Both girls jumped at the sound.

"Whoa!" exclaimed Lottie. "What do you think that is?"

"It is probably Mrs. Tygert calling us for breakfast."

"She could be the town crier. That's loud enough to wake all of Leadville."

The two of them hurried down the stairs. Sitting at the dining room table was a stern looking woman perhaps in her thirties. She was introduced as Miss Tilly Stiles, the high school English teacher.

Addie and Lottie were appointed seats across from each other. Tilly sat at one end and Anna Tygert at the other.

"Miss Stiles will say grace," informed Mrs. Tygert.

The Virginia girls folded their hands and bowed their heads while Tilly Stiles rattled off something that sounded more like an order than a prayer. They all added amen and breakfast was served: oatmeal, coffee and toast. Then Anna went to the kitchen and returned with a plate of cookies.

"We always enjoy cookies with our coffee in the morning. Don't we Miss Tilly?"

Tilly nodded and appalled the new onlookers by dunking her cookie into her coffee cup.

Exactly four cookies were offered, one for each, which chagrined Lottie, but she refrained from stating her dissatisfaction.

The landlady spoke. "I should have told you last evening that breakfast is at six forty-five sharp each morning except on Sunday. You may make your own from goods in the kitchen. I attend church services at St. George's Episcopal Church. You girls are free to come if you wish."

When they didn't answer right away, Tilly Stiles looked up and said, "You're not Catholic, I hope."

"There is the Annunciation Church," sang out Anna, trying to take the edge off Tilly's sharp remark.

"No," answered Addie. "We're non-denominational."

That answer brought a raised eyebrow from Lottie and a satisfied look from the other two.

"We have dinner at six o'clock sharp," said Tilly, after she wiped the remains of the soggy cookie from the edges of her mouth. "Tea is at two on Sunday afternoons. Now, I must hurry off to school. Oh, yes, the bathroom is mine from six to six- fifteen each morning."

Addie began to wonder if it was Anna Tygert or Miss Tilly Stiles who was in charge of the house.

After she left, a shy look came over Anna's kind, slightly wrinkled face. "Miss Stiles is punctual."

"She's bossy," remarked Lottie.

"I suppose it is a carryover from having to keep the high school children in hand." The landlady rose from her chair and began piling the soiled dishes.

"We can take them to the kitchen," offered Addie.

"Thank you but no. I like to handle my china and silver. They belonged to my mother. She carried them from Pennsylvania when she and Father moved out here. If you girls have time, I will show you the busy room."

"Busy room?"

Anna chuckled. "That's what I call it. That's the room with the washtubs, the ironing board, and the sewing machine."

Lottie's ears perked up. "You have a sewing machine?"

"It hasn't been used for a while. Not since my vision has deteriorated. You girls are welcome to use it, if you sew."

"Lottie is a whiz at sewing," complimented Addie.

They followed Anna Tygert into a large room that sat across the stair landing from the parlor.

"I do prefer that laundry is done only once a week. Water is precious in these mountains. In the spring and summer there is a clothesline out back. In the colder months we hang them in here. I keep the fireplace going and that helps to dry them." She chuckled again. "Of course they dry according to how well they've been rung out."

"When does Miss Stiles do her laundry?" asked Addie, positive that she would have a set time. It didn't seem prudent to infringe on Tilly Stiles.

"Saturday is her wash day," answered the landlady.

Addie looked at Lottie. "Let's do laundry on Wednesday. That way it will have plenty of time to dry before Saturday."

Lottie shrugged.

Anna Tygert clapped her hands together as though relieved that there would be no confrontation among her boarders. "Where are you young ladies off to today?"

"Job hunting," answered Lottie.

Anna smiled at them both. "That does sound exciting. I never had that opportunity."

Addie was enthusiastic. "We are looking forward to it."

Lottie looked at her in disbelief. Had her friend forgotten they were strangers who knew neither the town nor its people? To Lottie the prospect of looking for work gave her the jitters.

**

The young women assumed their luck would be better if they split up. They walked to Harrison Street where Addie crossed to the other side. She headed down the board sidewalk for the American National Bank they had passed when they stayed at the Delaware Hotel. Addie was good with numbers.

153

Lottie determined that she would stop in the first clothing store she saw. A seamstress might be needed in a place that sold clothes. She walked into M.B. Miller's store where inside the door she saw counters laden with linens, shirts and men's socks. They had no need for a seamstress but she might try the Golden Eagle.

Lottie found the store on Harrison Street. She told a clerk why she was there and was led to a small office. The office smelled of smoke. Shortly after taking a seat on an uncomfortable wood chair, the proprietor, Leopold Goldman, walked in smoking a cigar. Without a sign of greeting, he took a chair behind a small desk, picked up a piece of paper, read it, and turned to Lottie.

"So, you want a job as a seamstress?"

His brusqueness took her aback but she was quick to recover. "Yes, sir. My name is Miss Lottie Foster. I am newly arrived from Virginia, a high school graduate, and I have a talent for sewing."

He never hesitated. "Leopold Goldman." He nodded in her direction. "The pay is six-fifty a week. I have customers who expect the best. If you are good enough, the pay will go up to seven-fifty in two months."

Lottie sat for a moment, mulled over the offering, then said, "How about one month?"

The proprietor sat back in his chair and looked straight at her. Was she being too bold? He leaned forward and dropped his pencil on the desk. "One month. We open at eight, close at five-thirty on the weekdays, Saturday at four, closed on Sunday."

This was more than Lottie had hoped for. Apparently she didn't want to seem too eager. "I'd like to see where I'll be working before I agree."

He led her to an adequately sized room at the back of the store where a sewing machine was set up. Yard goods and sewing materials were stacked on a shelf. A full-length mirror placed on a short pedestal was an unexpected bonus. A round window sat above the sewing machine. Lottie looked out. All she could see was a mountain peak. She liked it. There were no shacks, ore smelters or irrigation ditches to ruin the view.

"When do I start?" she asked.

"Tomorrow. My other seamstress moved to my store in Denver. We're behind on alterations."

"Good," answered Lottie.

"Come on back to my office and fill out a paper. You be here a few minutes before we open at eight o'clock."

Lottie couldn't help but notice that Leopold Goldman never stopped either puffing or chewing on his cigar. Could she tolerate the habit?

Adelaide wasn't as fortunate in her quest for work. The bank only hired men, and she was not trained for the Mountain States Telephone and Telegraph Company. She wasn't yet desperate enough to try Adolph Hirsh's liquor store or the Board of Trade Saloon. Then she spied Davis Drug in a clapboard building. It was worth a try.

"May I help you, miss?"

A short man came from behind a stack of shelves.

"I am looking for a job."

"What kind of a job?"

"I'm not sure."

"We are a drug store, which means we sell medicines, bandages, ointments, that sort of thing. We also have a counter where we sell sandwiches, doughnuts, coffee, that sort of thing. Then we sell toothbrushes, toothpowder, mouthwash, that sort of thing."

Addie was beginning to think that being the salutatorian at her high school had not prepared her for any specific job.

"I'm very good with numbers."

"Are you good at measuring?"

"Measuring?"

"The miners are always coming in here with a note from the doctor wanting me to mix stuff together, an ounce here, a teaspoon there."

"Oh, yes sir!" said Addie. "Measuring is something I do very well."

The man scratched his balding head. "I'm getting busier all the time. Now that the gold business is picking up again these miners are always getting something. A cough here, a bruise there."

Addie couldn't help but smile. "I am very interested in a job."

"Tell you what." He pushed his spectacles up. "You can start tomorrow. Course you'll have to help with the food and wait on customers, but my eyes aren't what they used to be so I'll want your help to mix up some of this stuff they order."

Addie was so excited about finding a position that she almost forgot to ask. "How much does it pay?"

"Six dollars a week. Lunch is free. Open at eight and close at five-thirty. No work on Sunday and Saturday we close at five. They're all heading for the saloons about that time. What's your name?"

"Miss Adelaide Richards from Virginia."

"Well, Miss Richards, you be here tomorrow morning and we'll give it a go."

"Thank you, Mr...?"

"Davis, Bernie Davis."

"I shall look forward to it."

The girls met up in the afternoon. With great elation they talked about what they had accomplished. There was one problem. Rent included dinner and dinner was at six o'clock sharp. Could they make it from their work to Mrs. Tygert's by six o'clock for dinner? They could ill-afford to buy their own.

Chapter 25

Addie sat at the writing desk in the parlor. It was past time to send a letter to her parents. She would also pen a note to Clayton Lockwood. She had promised to write to him.

October 1, 1915

Dear Parents,

I regret that I have not written sooner, but I waited until Lottie and I were settled. I am pleased to report that we arrived safely without incident.

I cannot express in one letter the marvels we have seen. Once we crossed through the mountains of West Virginia, we saw the rolling hills of Ohio before the land seemed to flatten out. Fields of corn and wheat were in abundance and tiring. We were in awe when the train reached the enormous Chicago depot, but we found our way to the next train connection, the Denver & Rio Grande.

When we reached Denver, we were surprised to find it flat. This part of the country appears to be a series of plateaus, valleys and mountains. The air is thinner and drier than what we are used to. When I look toward the west, the view of the Rocky Mountains takes my breath away.

The hotel where we stayed in Denver was opulence in itself. They strive to give the easterners the luxuries they are used to. Of course, that does not mean Lottie and I growing up in the tenant houses. Denver is a busy stopping place for those going east and west.

Our final leg of the journey took us on a climb to this two-mile-high town. To say that we were disappointed with our first view of Leadville would be an understatement. A few of the buildings are grand and many are shacks. More people are coming because they are now dredging for gold. I assume they are hoping to strike it rich but most finds are bought out, and the old-timers around here don't expect the gold to last. They say they are used to people moving in and moving on.

As for Lottie and me, we met a very nice cowboy from Oklahoma named Caleb Dunn. He is familiar with Leadville and led us to this rooming house. A widow, Mrs. Anna Tygert, is the landlady. It is a modest Victorian, similar to some of the houses on Church Street in Berryville, with three bedrooms. She rents the two bedrooms she doesn't occupy, and we are free to use the rest of the house. Rent includes breakfast and dinner so we are saving money. Lottie and I are squeezed into one bedroom and a school teacher rents the other. We find her to be overbearing.

We have work. Lottie is working as a seamstress in a department store. I am working in a drug store. I help wait on customers, tend a small food bar and help the druggist with mixing medicines. Mr. Davis is pleased that I graduated high school. He says I am a fast learner and will learn much about medicine. I believe he is right.

159

I have rattled on enough. Lottie and I both think about home. For now, we will forge ahead and try to stick out one year. One never knows as circumstances always seem to change.

Hug the boys for me and kiss Sarah Jane. I do miss all of you.

My love,
Addie

She folded the letter neatly and placed it an envelope. Now, she would write the note to Clay and not have to think about writing for a couple of weeks.

October 1, 1915

Dear Clay,

This will be a quick note. Lottie and I are settled in Leadville. She has a job as a seamstress and I have one working in a drug store.

I trust you are enjoying the university. Have you decided on what path to take?

I am not sorry that I didn't go on to the normal school for teaching.

We live in a modest rooming house. There is a high school English teacher who also lives here. I wonder if I would become as sour as she seems to be if I had become a teacher. I don't care for her and neither does Lottie.

Speaking of Lottie, I think she is more homesick than I, but she is a trooper. I promised her a ticket home if she wanted to return. It will take me some time to save up the money because the trip here cost more than I planned.

160

I am learning to be on my own and I hope you are also.

Your friend,
Addie

She tucked the note into its matching envelope with a picture of a horse in the left corner. She smiled to herself as she thought of Clay. Then, she lamented the six cents in postage stamps she would spend to post these letters.

Lottie came down the stairs. "Caleb will be here in a few minutes, Addie. Are you ready to go?"

Addie turned in her chair. "Yes, I have written to my parents and to Clay. I should have done that last week. Have you sent a letter?"

"No. When your mother gets the one you wrote, she'll hurry on over to tell my mother and they will all be satisfied. I'll write in a few days. That way we are not wasting stamps."

"Are you being frugal or tight-fisted?"

"Don't forget, I have to buy my lunch, yours is free."

"Yes, but you earn fifty cents more a week."

"That doesn't buy much lunch. Hurry up. Caleb is borrowing the horse and buggy. I packed peanut butter sandwiches from the kitchen. Mrs. Tygert will be home from church soon. I do want to miss tea at two with Tilly Stiles bossing Mrs. Tygert around."

161

Addie rose from her chair. "You mean you want to miss the glaring eyes of Tilly Stiles."

"That woman gives me the creeps."

"If you'll get my cape, I'll run these letters upstairs. I'll mail them in the morning."

Lottie took Addie's long hooded cape off a coat rack.

Addie ran down the stairs with a pair of gloves in her hand, threw the cape over her shoulders, and said, "Let's go."

Caleb waited at the gate. He sat high on the seat of the buggy, which appeared to have seen some rough days. "I'd climb down and help you gals up, but this horse has a mind of its own. He might decide to go galloping off if I let go of the reins."

Lottie climbed up first surprising Addie with her show of swiftness and agility. Could it be that sitting next to Caleb was incentive enough?

Addie hesitated. "Do you think I should bring a blanket?"

"There's one in the back," said Caleb.

"Is it clean?"

"Clean enough if you get cold."

"Come on, Addie," urged Lottie. "I want to be gone before anyone gets back."

"All right." She took her seat next to Lottie. Caleb was quick to tap the horse and it took off in a lurch breaking into a fast trot.

Addie held onto her hat with one hand and grabbed the iron arm of the seat with the other. She noticed Lottie grabbed a hold on Caleb's arm.

Addie questioned, "Did this used to be a race horse?"

"Not that I know of. Belongs to my friend who loaned me the buggy. Think the horse just wants me to know he's boss when it comes to pulling this ugly thing."

Lottie chuckled. "It's good to know that someone is in charge."

"Where are we going?" asked Addie.

"I wanted to take you out and show you Turquoise Lake but it is five miles out and we didn't get an early start. So, I thought you might like to see the place my pardner and I bought when we were goin' to try fer gold."

They drove out of town and wound up a narrow dirt road. Addie was on the side of the seat where she could look at the sheer drop off the side of the road. Her grip was like iron. "Is this buggy safe, Caleb? Maybe we shouldn't be climbing up this steep grade."

"Scared?"

"No, cautious."

"We're about there."

As the horse had eased into a steady gait, Lottie had released her hold on Caleb's arm. "I'm beginning to feel equal to the top of these tall pine trees. Is that the only kind of tree that grows around here?" inquired Lottie.

"They've made a mess with the timber in these parts. There are aspens farther out. Mighty pretty about this time of year."

Caleb pulled the horse to a stop and tied the reins to a tree. Addie and Lottie climbed down off the uncomfortable buggy seat and stretched this way and that.

"I'm not looking forward to the trip back," said Lottie. "The ride up rattled every part of my body."

"Shucks, Miss Lottie. The ride down is a whole lot easier."

Addie saw a quick wink followed by a wide grin. Was Caleb Dunn getting sweet on her friend? That might be a reason for Lottie to stay in Leadville.

The young women were careful to hold their skirts well of the dirty ground. It seemed everything was dirt.

Caleb walked them to the entrance of the mine. "Want to go in?"

They peeked into the dark space and shook their heads.

"Have you found any gold?" asked Lottie.

"A little. We worked our way pretty far back, but my pal said it wasn't worth the effort. He went back home for ranchin'. He signed his part of the claim over to me and told me to do with it what I want."

"What are you going to do with it?" asked Adelaide.

"Hold onto it if I can. It's a right pretty spot with the stream flowin' by and the mountains behind. If I cut down a few more trees I think we could see forever."

After they walked around to admire Caleb's piece of the world, they entered the one-room mining shack. It contained a small blackened fireplace, a couple of wood chairs and a small table.

"It's dark in here," stated Addie.

"We leave the door open to let in the light." He laughed. "Course there's plenty of light comes through the cracks."

"Where do you sleep?" was Lottie's question.

"On the floor. I bring a bedroll. Now that Jess is gone, I sometimes come up here just to git away from town and the people."

"Lottie and I don't have much time to get around town."

"Maybe that's good. Lots of rough cobs down there drinkin' and gamblin' away all the money they worked fer. Some of the women are as rough as the men. It's the young girls I feel sorry fer. They come with starry eyes only to find themselves stuck in the saloons and bawdy houses." He must have read the stricken looks on the girls' faces. "Sorry fer such talk, that's just the way it is."

Lottie cleared her throat. "Caleb, I brought peanut butter sandwiches. Is there a place we can eat?"

He seemed relieved to have the subject changed. "You bet. We'll pull that blanket out of the buggy and go sit on the rocks near the stream. There's a little waterfall down the slope from here."

165

Caleb lifted the blanket from the buggy and shook it out. The two young women followed him to the restful spot where Addie, to her delight, found the blanket much cleaner than she expected.

Lottie doled out the sandwiches she had made and Addie surprised them with sugar cookies. "Mr. Davis said they would be stale by Monday so he gave them to me."

"How many?" asked Lottie.

"Enough for a snack before bed."

Lottie's face brightened. "I figure Mrs. Tygert is only going to have soup for our dinner when we get home."

She explained to Caleb. "Mrs. Tygert says that Sunday is her day of rest so dinner isn't much. For breakfast, the woman clangs a morning bell that's enough to wake the dead but tinkles a little bell for dinner." Lottie demonstrated with a little wiggle of her hand. "Soup's on, ladies," she sang out.

This brought laughter from all three. A release for the busy week they had just spent.

Chapter 26

The two young women were in a happy mood until they walked through the door of the rooming house. Anna Tygert was in a tizzy. She was fretting and wringing her hands.

"Oh, dear girls, I am at a loss. Miss Stiles and I sat down to tea and I found one of my silver spoons missing. We have been searching for it ever since."

"Maybe it fell under the rug," suggested Lottie.

"That is not the case, Miss Foster," chimed in Tilly Stiles, with her steely eyes looking directly at Lottie. "Anna and I have thoroughly searched the kitchen, the dining room, and the parlor. In the one full year I have lived here nothing like this has ever happened. Although, you are getting forgetful, Anna."

Addie snapped to attention. "You don't think we had anything to do with it, do you?"

If there was anything Anna Tygert disliked, it was consternation among her boarders. "Goodness, no. We will keep looking. You girls keep your eye out."

Tilly Stiles was silent, but Addie detected a smug expression on her face.

Addie and Lottie went to their room. "I'm steaming," said a disgruntled Lottie.

"No more than I. The nerve of that woman. I saw the way she looked at you, Lottie."

"Tilly Stiles and I have a mutual understanding. She doesn't like me and I don't like her."

They sat on the edge of their beds. "You shouldn't show it. Mrs. Tygert doesn't like friction in the house. Tilly has no reason to dislike you, has she?"

"I hardly know the woman. It wouldn't surprise me if she took Mrs. Tygert's spoon to blame it on us."

"Lottie, don't talk like that. We have to get along with the woman," said Addie.

"I wouldn't put it past her. Where are those sugar cookies? I need one to sweeten my disposition."

Addie got up from the bed and went to her dresser. "I put them in here."

"Check further," said Lottie, "maybe the silver spoon is hiding with them."

"That isn't funny. If you don't behave yourself, you can't have a cookie."

Lottie chuckled, " All right, Momma, I'll be good."

Addie laughed and threw the bag of cookies at her friend. "Catch."

Lottie reached up and snatched the bag. "Lucky I caught it. I don't like eating crumbs."

Addie sat on the bed. Lottie offered her a cookie, which she took and started nibbling on it. "I think Caleb likes you."

Lottie perked up. "What makes you think so?"

"I caught that wink and sly smile he sent in your direction."

"He was just being playful."

Addie lay back on the bed. "He didn't wink and smile at me."

"Jealous? He told us both he would come by next Sunday. Doesn't sound like someone who has an eye on me."

Addie looked over at her friend. "He couldn't very well just ask you, could he? He wants to take us out to see the Evergreen cemetery. That might be more excitement than I can take."

Lottie threw a pillow at her. "I'm crawling into my nightclothes. I hope Tilly isn't in the bathroom."

Addie sat up and threw her legs over the edge of the bed. "I'm going to suggest to Mrs. Tygert that she put a sign on the door so we can let someone know when it's occupied. I think Miss Stiles is the only boarder she has had besides us."

"What makes you think that?"

"When we were considering rooming here she didn't tell us when breakfast was served. She should have shown us where to do laundry, and she should have set down rules of the house, including use of the one bathroom."

Lottie was thoughtful. "I don't recall us asking."

"Just the same. If she was used to letting rooms, I would think there would be a list of rules.

And, what about her cat? Remember, Caleb said he retrieved her cat out of the bushes. She hasn't even mentioned a cat."

"Maybe it ran away. I don't see what that has to do with whether she has had any renters before us."

"It doesn't. I just happened to think about it."

Lottie shook her head. "You need to get some sleep."

**

At the breakfast table, Addie decided to ask Anna Tygert about the cat. She wasn't sure why she needed to know but she did.

"Mrs. Tygert, Caleb said he helped find your cat one day. Do you still have it?"

Anna put down her coffee cup. "My sweet Teddy. He was my companion after Mr. Tygert passed away. His favorite spot to curl up was in that rocker in the living room. At night, he slept at the foot of my bed. I do miss him."

"What happened to him?" asked Lottie.

"If I only knew. Teddy never left the house, and I don't know why he went out that day. It was good that Mr. Dunn happened by. It wasn't long after that my Teddy disappeared."

Tilly Stiles looked up. "Good riddance, I say."

A sad expression appeared on Anna's face but she didn't reply.

Tilly wiped her mouth with a linen napkin and announced she was off to school. Addie and Lottie had ten more minutes before they needed to leave.

"When did Mr. Tygert pass away?" Addie asked.

Anna offered a wan smile. "About a year and a half ago. It was six months after his passing I determined I would need extra money to keep my house going. Miss Stiles was like a godsend when she arrived and needed lodging."

"Have you had any other roomers?" asked Adelaide.

"One other lady, but she was only here for a month. I'm not sure she and Tilly hit it off."

"I can understand that," said Lottie.

"Mrs. Tygert, we need to be on our way. Is there anything you need from town?" offered Addie.

"No, dear, but it is kind of you to ask." Then she added, "I am so glad you girls decided to stay here. You bring youth and exuberance right along with you. I shouldn't say this, but Miss Stiles does not always look on the bright side of life."

Lottie chuckled. "That's for sure."

Anna Tygert watched as Addie and Lottie donned their long coats, placed their hats and started off to work.

Was there a wistful look in her eyes that said she wished she could do the same?

Chapter 27

Lottie liked her job at the Golden Eagle. Although this was only her third week, she enjoyed her solitary position. It was like being her own boss. Leopold Goldman gave instructions to the clerks not to bother Miss Foster. Although Lottie moved slowly, she worked fast. Leopold had bought the best Singer sewing machine, which lightened the burden. There was still plenty of hand sewing. Sometimes Lottie took work home if she was pressed for time. When Leopold's customers were happy, Leopold was happy. It looked sure Lottie would earn that dollar more a week by the end of her month's trial.

At Davis Drug, Adelaide looked out the front window onto the street. "Mr. Davis, who is that person?"

He peeked over the high counter where he was preparing a prescription. "Looks like "Baby Doe" Tabor. She lives out in an old shack at the Matchless Mine. Comes to town sometimes."

"She's dressed like a miner, boots, hat and all."

He came to stand next to Addie. "You've never heard of "Baby Doe"?"

Addie shook her head.

"You pass the big Tabor Opera House every day. That was her husband's money that built that, along with other buildings here and in Denver. He was one of the richest men in the country."

"What happened? She looks like a tramp."

They watched as "Baby Doe" crossed the street. "I'll try to make it short. Horace Tabor and his wife, Augusta, came out here from the East. They ran a store selling needed goods. He got lucky when he grubstaked a couple of prospectors and they struck it rich in silver."

"Where does "Baby Doe" fit in?"

"Horace was married but fell head-over-heels when he met her. His wife, Augusta, was an upright woman and wouldn't give him a divorce, so Horace set "Baby Doe" up in luxurious style in a posh hotel. Horace spent lavishly, hundreds of thousands of dollars at a time. When the government cut back on the silver they were buying, the price of silver plummeted. Horace went bankrupt. Augusta had given him a divorce earlier and he had married "Baby Doe". Horace died a few years after he went broke and supposedly told her to hold onto the Matchless Mine. I'm told she was a beautiful woman."

Addie was quick to speak, "She couldn't be too smart if she didn't hold onto some of that money."

Bernie Davis smiled as he went back behind the counter.

"What happened to Augusta?"

"Story has it she became a millionaire and moved to California."

"Smart woman," surmised Adelaide.

173

Bernie Davis laughed aloud. "If "Baby Doe" comes in, give her whatever she needs. The people in town try to keep her going."

The drug store was busy and Adelaide was glad to say goodbye when it was time to close. Lottie was waiting for her when she reached the department store.

"How was your day?" Addie asked.

"Overloaded. I met one of the wealthy ladies of Leadville and she wants me to make a dress for her for Christmas. Mr. Goldman ordered the expensive material. I hope I don't make any mistake in cutting out the pattern. It's an emerald green satin. She found the pattern in McCall's. Mr. Goldman said that if I mess up, the price of the material will come out of my pay."

"That doesn't seem fair."

"He's like that. I told him he'd better order plenty of material just in case."

Addie chuckled. "What did he say to that?"

"He told me I'd better get busy because I was wasting his money talking."

"He sounds like a hard-nose."

"I simply reminded him that he was in my work room, and he was the one who came in to talk to me."

They crossed to the other side of Harrison Street.

"Did he think you were being cheeky?"

"No. He chewed on his cigar, laughed, and said, "I'd better get out of here"."

174

They turned the corner and walked through the gate of the white picket fence.

Anna had just placed dinner on the table when the girls walked in.

She greeted them with a warm smile. "You're just in time. We have a lovely pot roast for this chilly evening."

"That sounds delicious," said Addie. "We both worked hard today."

Tilly Stiles occupied her usual place at the head of the table. "Nothing can be more draining than teaching school. Hurry up so I can say grace."

"We need to wash our hands."

"Then do so. Our food is getting cold."

"No, Tilly dear. It stays very warm in that covered pottery dish," advised Anna.

"They know that dinner is at six o'clock sharp. It is now five minutes after."

The girls ran their hands under the single tap in the kitchen and hurried back to the dining room.

Miss Stiles, once again, ordered the Lord to bless their food and they began to eat.

"Girls, the most wonderful thing happened today. I found my silver teaspoon in one of the drawers in the kitchen. I was sure that Tilly and I searched each drawer."

"Anna, I have told you before that you are getting forgetful," informed Tilly.

"I think any of us could make a mistake like that," said Addie.

"Anna is misplacing too many things. The other day I found her towels in my laundry. Last week we had to hunt up the key to the back door."

"Where did you find that?" asked Addie.

Anna spoke in a quiet voice. "It was in my apron pocket. I'm sure I looked there. I guess Tilly is right. I am getting forgetful."

Lottie said, "Mrs. Tygert. I think anyone could make those kinds of mistakes, especially when life is demanding. You do a very nice job of running the house even if Miss Stiles tries to run it for you."

Adelaide raised her eyebrows, Anna's expression changed to worry.

Tilly glared at Lottie, who never flinched. "I do not care for your impudence, Miss Foster."

Lottie answered, "I am not one of your pupils."

"Of course you are not. My students are taught manners."

Before Lottie could respond, Addie jumped in. "I believe what Lottie means is that none of us should forget that this is Mrs. Tygert's home and we are her guests."

Tilly turned her cold eyes on Addie. "I pay my way."

"As do we," Addie said. "That means use of the home, breakfast and dinner. It doesn't mean that we are allowed to order Mrs. Tygert about."

Tilly pushed her chair away from the table and left the room.

Anna was nervous. "Girls, I'm afraid you have upset Miss Stiles."

"Mrs. Tygert, we're sorry. We didn't mean to cause a problem, but I will be honest. In the three weeks we have lived here, Lottie and I have voiced concern about how Miss Stiles treats you. She had no right to talk to you the way she did. You are no more forgetful than any of us, and if we are to be reprimanded for being late for meals or anything else, that's your place to tell us not hers."

"She would probably be happy if we leave, as your other boarder did, but we don't plan on going," added Lottie.

Anna was at a loss for words except to say, "Let's have a piece of lemon pie."

Chapter 28

Wednesday of the next week, Addie returned from work to find two letters. One from Clay and one from her mother. She and Lottie hurried through dinner.

They lay on their beds up in their room where Addie opened the letter from her mother first. Lottie listened.

Dear Adelaide Mae,

We were glad to get your letter. I took it right over to read it to Mrs. Foster and she was glad to know that you and Lottie are both safe and well.

The boys want to hear all about what you have seen. I hope they don't get it in their heads to take off from home.

Your Pa is working hard. There is a lot to be done on the farm as you well know. Apples are in and there are plenty. We've wrapped some and put them in the barrels in the shed. They should keep for a good while if the rats don't get in there.

Sarah Jane is almost walking. She won't remember you when you come home.

Pa and the Fosters are happy to hear where you girls are working, but Pa said you girls are too smart to be saloon girls.

Nothing much has changed around here.

Love,
Momma

"I guess we haven't missed anything," mused Lottie. "Do you get homesick, Addie?"

"Sometimes. The mountains are pretty but I miss the trees and the hills and the green grass. If I am truthful with myself, I will say that I miss my family. Even that loft bedroom. How about you, Lottie?

"I miss the streets of Berryville where I knew almost everyone. It was comfortable. And the farm. That was comfortable, too."

Addie looked over at her friend. "Do you miss Sam?"

Lottie grinned. "No. When we got away from there, I realized what he was like."

"Want to hear what Clay has to say?"

"I'm all ears."

Addie wiggled into a comfortable position, tore open the envelope and began to read aloud:
Dear Addie,

It is the middle of October and I have been here at the university for six weeks. When your letter arrived, I sat right down and penned this reply.

I can't say your note was full of information other than you arrived safely and you and Lottie both have respectable positions. I didn't read that you are enamored with Leadville. I did some research on the place and found there were many notable people who got their start there or made millions off their investments: Marshall Fields, Carnegie, and Guggenheim to name a few. Even more interesting were the gunfighters who passed through. Zane Grey would be envious, although I suspect he passed through there also.

Do you still read those Western novels or has living there quenched your thirst for the West?

There is a School of Pharmacy here at the university. You should think about applying when you return. You will return, won't you?

I can't tell you how much it meant to me to see you this summer. Tell Lottie that I appreciated her keeping me up to date. She is a good friend to you. I suspect there is more to Lottie's personality than she allows to show through.

I am not sorry about that stolen kiss. Are you wearing the navy blue hat? I picture you, the hat and the kiss and drift right off to sleep.

Your friend always,
Clay

Lottie sat up. "Stolen kiss? Why didn't I ever hear about that?"

Addie folded the letter and put it back into the envelope. "Because it wasn't worth mentioning. He wanted to see the hats I bought from Miss Ramsburg. I tried on the blue one for him. He said to look right and left, then look straight at him, and when I did he kissed me."

"How romantic. If Clay kissed me I would have swooned on the spot."

"You wouldn't any more than I did. It was childish."

"What about his saying there is more to me than I let on. I can't imagine what he means," said Lottie.

"I can. I've never seen you stand up to people the way you have here."

Lottie smiled. "That's because I never met a Tilly Stiles or Leopold Goldman before. Let's go down and see if Mrs. Tygert has any leftover dessert."

Anna Tygert was in the kitchen washing her coveted china. There were tears in her eyes.

"Mrs. Tygert, what's wrong?" asked a concerned Addie.

"Oh, girls. I've done it again. Miss Stiles says that I absentmindedly dropped my hat in the hallway and she stepped on it and almost fell. I was sure I hung it up when I put my coat away. She says I need to go to a doctor to see what's wrong with me."

"I don't think there's anything wrong with you, Mrs. Tygert," said Lottie.

"Thank you, dear. I am beginning to worry."

"Do you remember hanging up your hat?" asked Addie.

"Not positively. I always hang it on the peg next to my coat. I cannot understand why I didn't this time."

"You probably did and it fell off," considered Addie.

Mrs. Tygert took her hands from the dish-water and rested them on the sink. "I doubt that's

181

possible because the hat has a hook of material in the crown that I secure over the peg. I am getting up in age. Oh dear, what if I am losing my faculties?"

"Any of these minor happenings are not cause to worry even if Miss Stiles tries to make them sound so. Do you have relatives: children, sisters, brothers?" asked Addie.

Anna Tygert went back to washing the dishes. "I have no one. Tilly has promised that she will take care of me if I get to the point that I can't do for myself. She is willing to take care of all my financial affairs."

"You should speak to a lawyer," advised Lottie.

"They are expensive. I just don't know."

"Mrs Tygert, I think Miss Stiles has you riled up for nothing. I might be able to get some legal advice for you and it shouldn't cost anything. Lottie and I think you are just fine, don't we Lottie?"

Lottie nodded her agreement. "Now, for the reason we came downstairs. Do you have any of those sour cream cookies left?"

Anna wiped her hands on a dish towel. "Of course I do. Right over here in this Teddy Bear cookie jar. I have decided to keep cookies in there for you girls for anytime you care to have them." She added, "Don't tell Tilly. This will be our little secret. Tilly says there should be no eating after meals are finished."

Lottie remarked, "That sounds like Miss Stiles is trying to be the boss again." She lifted the bear head of the cookie jar and helped herself to a cookie. "I have to hem some trousers. It's nice of you to take care of us the way you do," said Lottie.

"You brought work home again? It seems Mr. Goldman keeps you quite busy," observed Anna.

"He does, but I think I will be earning an extra dollar a week, so I don't mind. Addie can help me if I need it, then we can split the dollar."

"I like that idea," Addie said. "When did you decide that?"

"When I started on overload. I'm off to the busy room to hem those trousers. Thanks for the cookie, Mrs. Tygert."

"You are welcome, dear."

Anna turned to Adelaide. "Do you think you might get some legal advice for me? Mr. Tygert used to take care of all of our important business. First I lost him, then I lost Teddy. I don't want to lose my mind."

Addie felt pity for this little lady who was so good to her. She kissed her cheek. "Don't you worry. It might take some time. I'll get a letter off to a friend who knows a lawyer to see if I can get information. Don't make any rash decisions before I know."

"I promise."

Addie was pleased to see the release of a pinched expression on Anna Tygert's face.

**

When Sunday arrived, so did Caleb Dunn. He was in the same scruffy-looking buggy. Neither of the girls cared because they were glad to get away from the house and the town. Why Caleb had picked Evergreen cemetery for an outing they weren't sure

He was bright and cheerful. "Hi gals. I got the same horse and buggy. Climb on up.' They did as they were bid, Lottie next to Caleb and Addie next to Lottie. This time Addie prepared for the horse to take off by grabbing the front of the buggy with one hand and the handle of the seat with the other. Lottie, as before, latched onto Caleb's arm. Addie smiled to herself.

A short distance from town, Caleb drove the buggy under an arch that read: Evergreen Cemetery. He drove directly to a tombstone and said, "You gals read that name and see if you know who it is."

"You drove us out here to see a headstone?" asked Addie.

Lottie was at the stone and read aloud, "John B. (Texas Jack) Omohundro." She turned around with a quizzical look. "Is this supposed to mean something to us?"

Caleb came to where they stood holding tight to the horse's reins. "I thought it might. He wasn't from Texas at all. He was from Virginia, where you girls are from."

"Virginia is a big state," said Addie.

"I thought you might have heard about him. He was the one who started the Wild West Show. He was a friend of "Buffalo Bill" Cody and got him involved with it. Too bad for "Texas Jack" cause he died when he was thirty-three. Cody made a lot of money."

"This is kind of spooky standing over a grave and talking about somebody we didn't even know," said Lottie.

"Then climb back in the buggy. There's somethin' a bit farther up the lane you might like."

They did and were surprised to find a bandstand in the cemetery.

"Do they hold concerts here?" asked an incredulous Adelaide.

"On Decoration Day and the Fourth of July. Patriotic days when they honor the dead soldiers. It's quite an affair. I've heard them parading in with bagpipes. Gave me chills."

"Could we have lunch in the bandstand?" asked Lottie.

"Don't see why not. Did you bring somethin' good?"

"Would I not?" quipped Lottie, giving Caleb a coy smile. She picked up the small picnic basket.

Caleb surprised them when he pulled a guitar from under the blanket in the bed of the buggy.

"You gals get the grub ready and I'll sing you a few tunes. Guitar music is pretty out here in the quiet."

There was a bench in the bandstand where the young women sat to listen to Caleb sing along with his strumming. To their surprise they heard a mellow, pleasant voice. They happily listened to some cowboy ballads that were unfamiliar to them.

They ate egg salad sandwiches, drank tea and savored the remaining sour cream cookies from Mrs. Tygert's cookie jar.

"Caleb, it is peaceful out here. I liked your music. You have a very nice voice," complimented Lottie.

"Well, thank you Miss Lottie. Want me to show you how I can lasso?"

Addie gave Lottie a wry look and sideward glance. "What are you going to lasso out here? I don't see any cows," said Addie.

"You watch." He went to the buggy and pulled out a rope. After adjusting the noose so it satisfied him, he twirled it around his head, tossed it in the air, and lassoed a statue in the cemetery over twenty yards away.

Lottie was agog. "Caleb that's wonderful."

"I don't think the townspeople would appreciate you lassoing tombstones," admonished Addie.

"Shucks, no harm done."

He went to release the lasso while the girls were cleaning up the remains of their picnic. Lottie was folding up the blanket when two men rushed out from behind tall pine trees. It was obvious they were up to no good.

"Hurry up and get in the buggy," hollered Caleb still a distance away from the bandstand.

But before Addie and Lottie could get away, the men blocked their exit.

"You better get on your way," shouted Caleb as he hurried up.

"And leave these two pretty girls? We just want a little kiss."

Caleb reached the bandstand only to be slugged by the bigger of the two grungy looking men. "Get out of our way, boy." He hit Caleb again before he could get up from the ground leaving him stunned.

Addie and Lottie stood side by side. Trapped!

"Get out of here and leave us alone," shouted Addie in a shaky voice.

"Don't be skeered," said the shorter man as he stepped forward and took a hold of Addie. "Just a friendly kiss," he said, smiling to show his yellow teeth. His breath smelled of liquor and she tried to push him away. His smelly beard burned her cheek.

Lottie picked up the picnic basket and hit him over the head. Both men laughed and the one who clobbered Caleb barged inside only to be spun backwards by a rope. Caleb had gained his sense and lassoed the man. This distracted his friend, who was struggling with Addie. When he turned, Lottie threw the blanket over his head and she and Addie fought the squirmy mass until Caleb rushed in and carried him out. He had secured the bigger man on the ground with his rope and threw this second man next to him. Then he tied that man's feet together with the other end of the rope.

"You girls hurry into that buggy. They're not goin' to stay trussed up too long."

The girls were already on their way.

Seeing Lottie and Addie were in the seat, Caleb left the men on the ground and raced for the buggy. The horse took off like a shot. They lit out of the cemetery as though life depended on it. Maybe it did.

Addie and Lottie were shaking so bad they couldn't talk.

Caleb rubbed his swollen jaw. "Now, you gals see why it ain't wise to be out away from town by yerselves?"

They didn't answer; they were still recovering.

Lottie looked over at Caleb. "Your lip is bleeding and your jaw is swelling."

He pulled a bandana from his pocket and dabbed his mouth.

Addie said, "When we get to the rooming house you're coming in so I can put some medicine on your face."

"I can handle it. How about you two? Do you hurt any place?"

"My cheek burns, feels like I scraped it on a sidewalk," said Addie. "Otherwise, I'm all right. Lottie, you showed quick thinking throwing the blanket over that deranged derelict."

Lottie agreed. "Hitting him over the head with the picnic basket didn't do anything but ruin the basket. That was a cheap one a clerk in the store gave to me."

"Miss Lottie, I thought you did just fine."

"Caleb, you are supposed to call us Lottie and Addie."

He glanced at Lottie with a big admiring smile. "I'd be proud to."

When they reached the house, Addie insisted that Caleb come inside so she could dress his split lip and bruised jaw.

Anna Tygert was sitting in the parlor when they arrived. One look at Caleb's swollen face and Addie's red cheek caused her to rush from her chair.

"Oh my. What has happened?"

They gave her the hair-raising story as quickly as possible.

"And, that is why we made Caleb come in, so we can take care of his wound," informed Addie. "I have medicine upstairs."

Lottie, Caleb, and Anna went to the kitchen, where the women insisted Caleb sit at the small table. Addie returned with witch hazel and salve and found Lottie cleaning old blood off Caleb's face with a wet washcloth. Anna was a worried bystander.

Addie was applying salve to the cut on Caleb's lip when Tilly Stiles appeared in the doorway.

"What is all this ruckus?" she demanded. "I am trying to correct papers."

"Tilly, the girls were attacked at the cemetery and Mr. Dunn saved them from peril."

"Most likely you were up to something you shouldn't have been doing." Her eyes danced from Addie to Lottie.

"We went on a picnic before it gets so cold that we can't go," answered Addie. "Two hidden drunk ruffians came out of the pine trees."

"Are you sure you didn't entice them?"

"Now ma'am," interjected Caleb, "these are respectable young women and you have no call to talk to them like that."

"I'll talk to them any way I please." She turned on her heel and mumbled something that sounded like, " Temptresses, the both of them."

Lottie was ready to speak her mind but Addie placed a steady hand on her arm. It wouldn't do to upset Mrs. Tygert any more than they already had.

Caleb rose from his chair holding his tall cowboy hat in his hand. "Thank you fer doctorin' me up, and Mrs. Tygert, thank you fer lettin' me come in banged up as I was. I sure am sorry today turned out the way it did."

"The day ended up fine. It was just the middle that was a little scary," said Lottie.

"You are all fine and that is what counts," said a grateful Anna. "I'm sure Miss Stiles was short because of the work she needs to have ready for school tomorrow. We do have to understand that she has a demanding job."

"Where does she come from?" asked Addie.

"Nebraska. I'm not sure it was a happy place for her. She is a good person."

Addie and Lottie eyed each other. They weren't so sure.

Chapter 29

In early November, Addie received a letter from Clay in response to one she had written to him asking if his brother, Alex, would give her some legal advice. Addie wasn't sure why, but she felt Alex owed her something. Perhaps because he had caused her mother angst. Helping Laura's daughter may be some compensation.

Clay was to the point. He wrote that if she wanted something from Alex she should ask him herself. Aggravated by his terse reply, she blamed herself for not having done so in the first place. She had wasted time.

Addie could send a Western Union telegram. Did she dare spend the money? Would Alex think there was an emergency if she sent a telegram? She had only met the man once. Maybe he would think it was a prank? Although, who would pay good money to send a prank telegram?

Addie thought she should consult with Lottie and then she thought not. It was her idea and she might as well follow through with it.

The next day, Addie asked Bernie Davis if she could have fifteen minutes to take care of personal business. He said to go ahead as long as it didn't take more than fifteen minutes.

On the way to the telegraph office she changed her mind. The operator in the Berryville office would see it and that may become a problem. Privacy wasn't always the policy in a small town. She decided telephoning was a better choice as long as she chose her words carefully.

Addie went into the Mountain States Telephone and Telegraph Office. The long distance operator gave her the number of the Lockwood Law Office. Her heart jumped into her throat when she heard it ring; then she heard his voice.

"Alexander Lockwood."

The operator broke in, "You have a long distance call from Adelaide Richards. Will you accept it?"

Addie held her breath. Would he accept the charge for the call?

A few seconds hesitation on his part and then, "Yes," was his response.

"Go ahead Miss Richards," said the operator.

Before she could speak, he asked, "What's the problem, Adelaide? Are you in trouble?"

He knew who she was. So far, so good.

"No, I'm not in trouble. I live in a rooming house in Leadville, Colorado run by an elderly lady. She needs legal advice and can't pay a lawyer."

"There is a reason you called me?"

"You're the only lawyer I know. I wrote to Clay and asked if he would talk with you. He said if I needed something I should ask you myself. She is a lovely lady. I thought you could give me some advice for her."

"What does it concern?"

"I'd rather not say over the phone."

"Send me a letter."

"That would take too long."

"Adelaide, how do you expect me to give you advice if I don't know the reason?"

This wasn't going well. For a smart girl she sounded like a dimwit. Addie's heart sank.

She heard an exasperated sigh over the phone. "Did you know I will be addressing the Colorado State Bar in Denver in a couple of weeks?"

"How would I know that?"

"You've been in touch with Clay. He might have told you." Was he annoyed?

"I'm sorry I called."

He was quick to say, "Wait, don't hang up. If you think this is serious enough to call me, then I would like to help. What if I come to Leadville once I've delivered my address?"

"But, that will cost you more money, and it is out of your way."

"Do you want me to come or not? That's the only way I can get a handle on what's going on."

"Oh yes. I want you to come. We can't pay you, and it is a long train ride from Denver."

"Those are my concerns. It might be good for me to get away for a while. I will send you a note when to expect me. Goodbye, Adelaide."

"Goodbye, Mr. Lockwood."

Addie wanted to jump for joy. She couldn't believe her good fortune. Alex Lockwood was coming to Leadville. Life was good.

Then she wondered why Alex would spend that kind of time and money to come and help someone he didn't know. Certainly, she knew. For the same reason she felt she should call him. He was trying to make up for the unhappiness he had caused her mother when they were young.

Back at the drug store, Addie kept checking the watch Clay had given to her for a graduation present. She was aching to tell Lottie her news.

"You're antsy today, Miss Richards," observed Bernie Davis.

"I have a lot on my mind. Look, here comes Mrs. Rhoden with a paper in her hand." She lowered her voice. "I'll bet the doctor has given her another prescription for those placebo pills she thinks work."

"Miss Richards, be careful what you say," he admonished her.

The bell tinkled when the woman opened the door. Addie went to greet her. "Hello, Mrs. Rhoden, we haven't seen you for a couple of weeks."

"Hello, Adelaide. My lumbago has been acting up something awful. You know I get rid of one thing and then I get another. I have a new medicine the doctor wants me to try. He says they are the best for my ills."

Addie took the prescription to the druggist.

"It will take me a few minutes," he said.

That seemed all right with Mrs. Rhoden. "Adelaide, I would like to have a cup of coffee and one of those fancy powdered doughnuts."

Addie was cheerful, "Coming right up."

195

"It will take me a few minutes to get to the chair. It is so difficult to walk. I was sure I was having a heart attack the other day but the doctor says my heart is fine. And I still have the headaches and my kidneys are going bad. I'm in bad shape, Adelaide."

Elsie Rhoden plopped her heavy bottom onto a chair. She took a sip of the coffee and sighed. "This helps to soothe my throat."

There was no problem with her appetite, Addie noticed, because she devoured the doughnut in four bites.

"These are delicious. Did you make them, Adelaide?"

Addie was washing powdered sugar off the counter. "No, ma'am. Mr. Davis hires Mrs. George to make them."

Elsie Rhoden turned up her nose. "You mean that Indian woman?"

"Yes. You said the doughnuts were delicious."

"I guess I did. She's one Indian who is good for something."

Addie scrubbed the counter with a little more force.

Bernie Davis pressed a buzzer that told Addie the prescription was ready. She went to pick up the bottle.

"Bernie whispered in her ear. They're green this time. Same stuff."

Elsie Rhoden opened her pocketbook to pay for the pills and the snack. She looked at the price on the bottle. "Fifty cents!" she exclaimed.

"The directions are to take one in the morning and one at bedtime," informed Adelaide. "This bottle should last for a couple of months."

"I do hope so."

.Elsie Rhoden picked her cane off the back of a chair and limped out the door.

Addie smiled as she watched her cross the street. "She reminds me of a woman back home," she said. "If she couldn't complain about some physical ailment, she wasn't happy."

Bernie Davis shook his head. "It takes all kinds to make a world, Miss Richards."

Addie was beginning to find that out.

Chapter 30

Lottie Bell Foster was humming to herself as she sat in her sewing room in the Golden Eagle department store. Caleb had taken her to a town dance last Saturday night. Addie stayed at the rooming house. She said she had letter writing to do.

Caleb danced with Lottie almost every dance. Although she found a lot of men to be nice, she found Caleb to be extra nice. Addie said he was too much of a showoff and immature acting. Lottie didn't think so. Caleb didn't try to pretend he was someone he wasn't, like some young men she had met.

Lottie finished her alterations for the day and was wearing white cotton gloves to work on the emerald green satin. She didn't want any smudgy fingerprints on the material. If the dress was finished by Thanksgiving, the woman who ordered it could come in and carry it home. The sooner the dress was out of her hands the better, thought Lottie.

Leopold Goldman tapped on the door before he opened. It unusual for Leopold because he owned the store and was used to doing as he pleased.

"If you've got that cigar in your mouth, don't come near me," warned Lottie. "I don't want ashes to fall on this dress. It will cost you a bundle of money to start all over." She knew the mention of spending money always caught his ear.

"So, are you going to have it made in time?"

She stopped sewing and looked over at him. "If I don't keep getting interrupted," she answered.

The short, stooped little man stood in the doorway chomping on his cigar, a shock of gray hair falling on his forehead. "I just got a bunch of material in that I didn't order. Looks like Christmas stuff all red and green. What do you think I should do with it?"

Leopold was asking her?

"Sell it to people."

"This town is full of miners, not likely they're going to buy it."

"What did you have in mind, Mr. Goldman?"

"I thought you could make some blouses, skirts, that sort of thing."

Did he realize what he was suggesting? "I am only one person. There's only so much I can do."

"When you've got the time, you come out and look at this stuff." He turned and shut the door.

Lottie would look at it before she left for the day, but she knew there was no time to make blouses and skirts before Christmas.

Lottie looked out the window at the mountain peaks covered with snow. The weather was getting cold. She wondered if it snowed more here in Leadville than in her native Virginia. She

199

had missed the changing leaves and harvest time and November was beginning to look bleak. At home, she would be up in her room working on something for her parents for Christmas. But, she wasn't home. She had promised Addie a year and hoped she could keep her promise.

When it was quitting time, Lottie went to see the material that had arrived without Leopold having ordered it. It came from a friend of his in the fabric trade. Lottie wondered why everyone didn't stick together and help each other out as the Jewish people did.

Addie was waiting when Lottie came out of the shop. "What took you so long? We're going to be late for dinner."

"I had to check some material for Mr. Goldman. I don't care if we're late. It's Tilly who wants dinner at six o'clock sharp, not Mrs. Tygert."

"Yes, but Tilly has a way of sending our landlady into a tizzy."

The sun set a lot earlier these days so they hurried up Harrison Street in the dusk.

"Lottie, listen to this. I called Alex Lockwood today and he is coming here to talk with Mrs. Tygert."

Lottie stopped in her tracks. "Clay's brother? All the way from Virginia? I don't believe it."

Addie took her arm and urged her on. "Believe it. He said he will speak in Denver to the Colorado State Bar, then he will come out here after he does."

"Why would a small town lawyer be invited to speak way out here?"

"Clay said Alex used to work in Washington and knows a lot about how the government works. Maybe that's why. I don't care as long as he comes."

"When will that be?" asked Lottie.

"I'm not sure. I think in a couple of weeks. He said he would send a note."

"I still don't understand why he would come all this way?"

"He owes it to my mother!" came Addie's sharp reply.

Lottie offered a wry look. "I'm not even going to ask why."

They turned the corner and hurried through the white picket fence of the rooming house.

"We're sorry we are late," called Addie. "We will be in as soon as we wash our hands."

When they sat down, Tilly Stiles was eating her meal. "Late again," she said, without looking up. "You missed grace."

"We hurried as fast as we could," advised Addie. "Mr. Goldman needed Lottie for a few extra minutes."

"Girls, your food is still warm. I had to put it all together in my pottery dish but it will still taste good."

Anna lifted the top of the large pot to reveal pork chops, potatoes and turnips.

It was difficult to tell the taste of the potatoes from the turnips, but Addie and Lottie were hungry so they didn't care.

"I made apple grunt for dessert."

"With hard sauce?" asked Lottie.

"Oh yes, dear. It wouldn't be right without it."

Tilly rose from her chair. "Anna, how many times have I told you that it isn't healthy to have dessert every night?"

Anna's eyes were downcast. "I know, but I do like to bake and these young girls need a little something extra."

"You coddle them," she said, and left to go upstairs.

Addie and Lottie were busy finishing their dinners. "Mrs. Tygert you can bake all you like. There is nothing like dessert after dinner," said Addie.

"Or any other time," enjoined Lottie.

They all laughed.

Chapter 31

Lottie found there was a reason for the free material Leopold Goldman received from his friend. The friend was really his brother-in-law who lived in a highly populated Jewish neighborhood in New York City. It wasn't likely the Jewish people would buy anything related to Christmas. Why did the brother-in-law think a town loaded with miners would be any different? Could it be he had something against Leopold?

Lottie was in the sewing room at the store.

"Been thinking what you can do with all that stuff?" Leopold asked her as he pointed his cigar toward the heap of gifted material piled on the floor.

"Yes," she replied. "I've been talking with Addie. We think we can make some items that will sell. Our landlady said we can bring the material to the house so we can work on it in our spare time. Would you mind if we used some of the cloth for ourselves?"

He chomped his cigar, mulling this over before he answered, "Whatever you can sell in the store will be extra money for me. Use what you need for yourselves."

"Thank you, Mr. Goldman. That's generous of you."

"Now, I didn't say you can have it all."

Lottie smiled, "I think you will be pleased."

The bolts of material in Christmas colors were plain, plaid and striped patterns in cotton, flannel, corduroy, and one bolt of taffeta. Lottie's head was swimming with the possibilities.

**

On Saturday, Caleb came into town with the loaned buggy and carried Addie, Lottie and the bolts of cloth to Mrs. Tygert's boarding house.

Anna was excited when they arrived. She held open the door to the busy room as the three carried the materials in. "Oh my, look at all those beautiful colors. We are going to have such a good time putting this together."

Addie and Lottie were skeptical, but the venture put a happy smile on Anna's face giving them pleasure.

That evening, at the dinner table, they talked about what they could make to sell for the Golden Eagle and for themselves.

Addie spoke, "An idea came to me that we can make gifts for our families. When Alex Lockwood comes, he can take them back for us."

Tilly's head snapped up. "Who is he?"

"A friend from Virginia," answered Addie, sorry she had let the cat out of the bag.

"Why is he coming?"

"He has business in Denver. He plans on extending his trip and will stop to see Lottie and me."

"Is he a romantic acquaintance?" Tilly was full of questions.

Addie met her eyes. "No. He is a friend of my mother's. I think he is interested in our welfare and will report back to our parents."

It was doubtful Tilly accepted that explanation, but she resumed eating.

Addie said, "To get back to what we can make with the material we have, I am thinking Christmas stockings."

Lottie agreed. "They would work with the corduroy. I wondered about bandannas, nightgowns and handkerchiefs for the cotton and flannels."

Anna spoke in a quiet voice. "Lace trimmed doilies would be pretty."

Tilly sat taking in the conversation. "Thanksgiving is next week. It's foolhardy to think you can accomplish much before Christmas. I don't want that work room filled with junk."

Lottie spoke in an even voice, "I don't believe it is your room."

Tilly glared at her.

Anna began to twitter. "Oh dear, dear. Tilly we will be sure that you have your space."

"See that you do," she said. "Anna, you left a skillet of grease on the hot fire this morning. If I hadn't come into the kitchen, you could have burned the house down."

205

Anna's hands went up to frame her face and she shook her head. "Oh my, no! How could I have done that? I don't recall cooking anything with grease this morning."

Tilly stood up. "That's just it. You don't remember." She stalked off and went up the stairs.

"Mrs. Tygert, did you fry up bacon this morning?" asked Lottie.

Anna sat with a blank look on her face. "I fry bacon many mornings. When I do, I am careful to remove the pan from the heat. At least, I think I am."

"Has Miss Stiles said anything more about taking over your affairs?" asked Addie.

"She is willing to. I am beginning to think it might be the best for me. Think of it, I could have burned down the house! I am becoming careless."

"We don't know if that's true," said Addie. "Mrs. Tygert, Alex Lockwood is a lawyer. I asked him to come because Lottie and I both think Miss Stiles is playing some kind of a game."

"A game? Tilly doesn't play games."

Addie didn't try to explain. "Please talk with Mr. Lockwood when he comes."

"But, dear girl, how can I afford to pay him?"

"We have an understanding. There will be no cost to you."

Anna fretted, "Why is it that our exciting day has gone downhill?"

"I know the answer," said Lottie. "Tilly Stiles!"

Addie wagged her head at Lottie. "Mrs. Tygert, while you are washing up the dishes, Lottie and I are going to make a list of what we can put together for Christmas. We will need your ideas, so be sure and come in once you're done in the kitchen."

"Do you girls think I can be of any help?"

"You certainly can," said Lottie. "We may make you work so hard that you'll wish you had never seen all that pretty cloth."

Anna smiled and began clearing the table.

As the girls prepared for bed that evening, Addie looked over at her roommate. "I saw you and Caleb holding hands when you walked him to the buggy. It was good of him to help us out. Do you like him a much as you liked Sam?"

"I like him more than I liked Sam. We had a fun time that night he took me dancing. He wants to take me to the cinema, but now that we have that work to do before Christmas, I don't want to waste the time."

Addie pulled her nightgown over her head. "It doesn't sound like a waste of time to me. We don't have any timeline except to be sure we have our gifts ready for Alex Lockwood to carry home."

Lottie sat on the edge of the bed unlacing her ankle-high shoes. "That's true. When do you think this Lockwood lawyer will arrive?"

Addie climbed under warm covers. "I wish I knew. Maybe after Thanksgiving. We'll lose another day's pay."

"We can use the day to cut out patterns. I hope Mrs. Tygert lets us help with Thanksgiving dinner. My mother and I always worked together. Pies were my specialty."

Addie groaned. "I helped with everything. It was two days of preparation and twenty minutes of eating."

Lottie laughed. "But, the fun was picking at everything after dinner was over."

"Don't get homesick thinking about it. I'm bushed," said Addie. "Good night, Lottie."

"Night, Addie."

Chapter 32

Saturday night, Lottie went to the cinema with Caleb. Addie used the time to work on gifts for her family. When he came to the house that evening, Mrs. Tygert invited him for Thanksgiving dinner. He accepted, which pleased Lottie.

There was one wrinkle that needed to be ironed out. Alex Lockwood had sent a note that he would arrive on the 4:32 p.m. Denver & Rio Grande train on Wednesday evening. This caused Addie discomfort because he hadn't said how long he would be in town. There had to be time for him to talk to Mrs. Tygert alone. And, she wanted him to meet Tilly Stiles.

What she did was ask Anna Tygert if Alex could be a guest for Thanksgiving. Anna was all for it. "Six of us for dinner? I will be able to use all of Mother's silver and china."

Addie planned to meet Alex when he arrived and hoped he would accept the invitation.

She and Lottie had been busy crafting the gifts for their families. They made tea cozies for their mothers, neckerchiefs for Addie's brothers, men's handkerchiefs for their fathers and Anna had made a small rag doll for Sarah Jane. She dressed the doll in a long red and white striped cotton dress with a bonnet to match. The gifts could easily be tucked into a suitcase.

Much thought had been put into Christmas items they could make for the Golden Eagle. Caleb thought the neckerchiefs and men's handkerchiefs would sell. Out of red checked material, Mrs. Tygert had sewed a sample of a tobacco pouch with a drawstring top. Caleb snatched it up and tested the drawstring by pulling it closed with his clenched teeth. He declared it was right fine. If those items passed approval from a cowboy, then the young women were satisfied. Men were not likely to part with their money unless it was for alcohol and tobacco.

Mrs. Tygert enjoyed making rag dolls and doilies. Addie and Lottie cut patterns for nightgowns for women and children. Addie had figured out a way to make hair bows for girls. Lottie was going to attempt to make a few small vests for young boys. There would be plenty to keep them busy once Thanksgiving was over.

Wednesday arrived and Addie was a bundle of nerves. Bernie Davis allowed her to leave an hour early. She had to hurry to get to the railroad depot or she might miss Alex. The train wasn't always on schedule. Please let this be one of those times.

It wasn't difficult to pick him out of the few passengers standing on the platform. He wore a derby hat, double-breasted camel hair overcoat, leather gloves and carried a briefcase. He was waiting for his luggage.

Addie was breathless. "Mr. Lockwood?"

He turned and smiled at her with those same warm brown eyes she remembered from when she met him in the stables.

"Adelaide."

"I ran all the way from the drugstore. I was afraid I would miss you."

"I would have waited," he said. "I need your help in getting to a reputable hotel. I'm trusting they are not all filled with holiday visitors."

"I'm sure that isn't the case. "We have the Delaware, Clarendon, and Windsor."

"Which one is closest to your rooming house?"

She was quick to reply. "That would be the Clarendon. It is expensive."

"They are all expensive," he answered.

"Not the ones down around Second Street. That's the seamier side of town."

Alex chuckled. "You have grown to become a woman of the world."

"I have learned to be aware of my surroundings."

The porter brought his suitcase and Alex rewarded him with a coin. Addie was pleased to see that the case would hold the Christmas gifts she and Lottie wanted to send home.

"How is everything in Virginia?" she asked, half as a way of making conversation.

"Fine when I left."

"Have you seen my family? I disappointed my mother when I didn't go away to become a teacher."

211

He looked at her. "I run into your father and your brothers when I get a chance to get out on the farm. I haven't seen your mother since before you went away. That time, our paths crossed by chance. I advised her to let you go. You have to live the life you choose."

His words gave her a warm feeling. "I know the story about you and my mother when you were young."

He didn't look at her this time. "Those are the words, Adelaide. We were too young."

There was a finality in his tone that made her glad. She had been afraid when he moved back to the farm that it might rekindle a spark. His manner assured her that her worries had been for naught. She had pushed that fear to the back of her mind for months. The release lifted her soul.

"Mrs. Tygert, our landlady, would like to have you come for Thanksgiving dinner tomorrow."

He was pleased. "I wondered how I was going to spend the day," he said. "I would be honored to come."

"We will all be happy. There will be six of us and a good place for you to be introduced to everyone. You haven't asked the reason and I haven't told you why I wanted you to come."

"Wait, don't tell me. I want to get a feel for this place before you do."

They had walked up the wooden sidewalk of Harrison Street and stood in front of the Clarendon Hotel.

"A most impressive opera house we passed. Have you been to performances?"

She laughed. "I don't earn the kind of money to squander away at the Tabor Opera House."

"Perhaps we can take in a show while I'm here."

"How long will you be staying?"

"That all depends on how much time it takes to iron out your concerns."

Addie blushed with embarrassment. "I just realized what an awkward position I put you in. Can you forgive me?"

"That all depends," he said.

"On what?"

"On you giving me the address so I can show up for dinner."

"Oh, my goodness. Of course." She reached into her coat pocket and pulled out a piece of paper. "I've written the address, and dinner is at two in the afternoon.

"I'll be there. Should you be walking home in the dusk by yourself?"

"It's almost around the corner. I might run into Lottie on her way home."

"The girl who came with you?"

Addie smiled and took his gloved hand. "Yes. You'll meet her tomorrow. Thank you so much for coming."

She turned and hurried down the street.

Alex stood and watched her go before he went through the glass double doors of the Clarendon Hotel.

213

**

Alex wrapped on the door of Anna Tygert's rooming house. Addie wore her Sunday dress. It was her white graduation dress but Lottie had fashioned an overskirt of brown plaid and a jabot of the same material. She wore the watch pin Clay had given her and fashioned her honey-colored hair with a bow.

She and Lottie had both had a hand in preparing dinner.

On her way to the door, Addie removed the white bib apron that was stained from kitchen work before she opened the door.

"Mr. Lockwood. It is so good of you to come." She took his coat and hat and hung them on the coatrack at the foot of the stairs. "We will be putting the dishes on the sideboard, shortly. Before we do, I would like to introduce you to our party."

They stood in line to greet him as though he was President Wilson, himself.

"Mrs. Tygert, I would like you meet Mr. Lockwood." Anna smiled as he nodded. "Mrs. Tygert owns the house," said Addie. "And, this is Miss Stiles." Tilly looked him squarely in the eye. "Miss Foster, perhaps you remember her from the farm. And, Mr. Dunn." Alex and Caleb shook hands.

"I am pleased to meet all of you. Mrs Tygert, I thank you for inviting me to dinner. Now, I ask that you call me Alex. It is much more comfortable for me."

Tilly Stiles became in charge. "Then you must call us by our given names. Mine is Matilda. Welcome to Leadville."

"I'm Lottie. Although we haven't met, we live on the same farm. I do know your brother, Clay."

Alex took her hand. "It is unfortunate that we haven't met sooner. I know I have heard Clay mention your name." Those words pleased Lottie.

Caleb stuck out his hand again and Alex clasped it. "I sure am glad we got the stuffy part out of the way. I'm Caleb Dunn from Oklahoma. I'm lookin' forward to a big dinner."

Alex laughed. "So am I."

"Now, girls, you may help me bring in the dishes of food, Tilly can show Mr. Lock...Alex, and Caleb their places at the table."

The two young women followed Anna to the kitchen while Tilly seemed more than pleased to usher the men to the dining room table bedecked with a white crocheted table cloth and set with the cherished china and silver.

Caleb furnished the wild turkey that Mrs. Tygert carved and placed on a big platter. Gravy, dressing, mashed potatoes, winter squash, green beans, slices of baked bread and cornbread were placed on the sideboard.

They took their places at the table and Tilly said grace, "Dear Lord, we thank you for these gifts of nourishing food and for the gathering of guests at this table."

Addie and Lottie looked at each other across the table. This was the most thankful and undemanding grace they had heard from Tilly. Usually there was a lengthy something about ordering the wrath of God to be brought down upon these sinners.

The food was passed until everyone took their portion.

"You gals have really dished up a fine plate of grub," said Caleb.

"Mrs. Tygert did most of the work," said Addie. "I made the bread and baked apples. Lottie made the mincemeat and pumpkin pies…"

"And, we all peeled the potatoes, squash, and snapped the beans," Lottie finished the sentence.

Alex smiled at Tilly. "What was your part?" he asked.

Was there a faint blush on that flinty face? "Anna allows me to care for her silver and china. I was in charge of setting the table."

"I believe you have outdone the Willard Hotel in Washington. My compliments."

"Thank you. Tell us about your home in Virginia. I have never been to the East."

Alex buttered a piece of bread. "Although we are east of here, we consider ourselves from the South. Richmond is much different from Philadelphia, Boston, and New York City. I have recently returned to live where I was born in Clarke County. The same place Adelaide and Lottie are from. Before that, I spent time in Washington and Richmond."

"What brings you out here?" asked Tilly.

"I had a speaking engagement in Denver. I came to Leadville to see firsthand how these young women were faring so I can carry the news to their parents. It was quite an undertaking on their parts to travel all this way."

Tilly's praise was a surprise. "I should say so. Adelaide and Lottie seem to be strong young women. Their presence has brightened the house."

At that point, Anna Tygert rose from her chair. "I do believe it is time to bring in dessert."

"Lottie and I will bring in the pies," said Addie. "You've done enough work for one day."

She heard Alex ask Tilly, "Are you a relative of Mrs. Tygert?"

Tilly Stiles offered a sweet smile. "Not a blood relative. I teach English at the local high school. Anna has been wonderful to allow me to rent a room. We have become very close, haven't we, Anna? Almost like mother and daughter."

What could Anna do but nod her head.

Addie gritted her teeth as she went into the kitchen. She whispered to Lottie, "Did you hear what she said?"

"She isn't acting like the Tilly we know."

"No, she isn't. Let's take the pies in."

"And throw one in her face," said Lottie.

Addie gave a loud sigh, "If we only could."

When dinner was over, both Caleb and Alex announced they had to be on their way.

Tilly addressed Alex, "Will we be seeing you again?"

"I hope to be in town for a few days," he answered. "It has been a pleasure to meet you, Matilda, and everyone else."

Addie handed him his coat and hat and followed him out the door. Lottie was standing at the buggy, seeing Caleb off.

"Alex, when am I going to see you alone? We need to talk."

"How about Saturday night? John Philip Sousa's band is presenting a concert at the Tabor Opera House. You said you've not gone."

"I haven't anything grand to wear."

"Wear what you have on. You can tell me what brought me out here, and we will be entertained by an evening of great music."

Addie was reluctant. "I know we can't discuss this at the rooming house or at the drug store where I work. If it has to be the opera house, then I'll go."

"Good. Tomorrow I don't plan on doing anything but resting up. I'll pick you up at seven o'clock on Saturday evening."

That was fine with Addie. She went back into the house where Lottie and Anna Tygert were cleaning up. Tilly Stiles had disappeared into her upstairs room.

"Poor Tilly has developed a headache," informed Anna. "Otherwise, she would be helping with the clean-up."

Lottie groaned. "Always an excuse when there is work to be done. I'd like to give her a headache."

"Lottie, dear. You must be charitable," cautioned Anna.

Chapter 33

Saturday evening, Lottie was helping Addie get dressed for her big outing at the opera house. Lottie decided the bolt of plaid taffeta, the free cloth Leopold Goldman had received, would make an appropriate addition to Addie's wardrobe. They sewed into the late hours on Friday to finish an ankle-length skirt for the Saturday performance.

Mrs. Tygert was excited when Addie told her where she was going. From her room she carried a cream-colored lace, long sleeved blouse with a high neck and ruffled bodice. She also brought a fur wrap. "Mr. Tygert and I went to the opera house many times. After he passed, I tucked these away thinking I would never use them again."

"Mrs. Tygert, I would be afraid that something would happen to them if I wore them."

"No, my dear. I want you to have these. If something happens to them, I will just be happy that they were worn to the Tabor Opera House one more time. I have no use for these anymore."

Addie washed the blouse and Lottie had to make a couple of adjustments, but the lace was a perfect complement to the red, green and cream plaid taffeta skirt.

They were upstairs in their room. Lottie was finishing a spot on the hem.

"I'm a nervous wreck," announced Addie. "I was all thumbs at the drug store, and I almost spilled soup on a customer. Mr. Davis made a comment about how I wasn't my usual self."

"What did you tell him?" asked Lottie, removing a straight pin from between her lips.

"I told him the truth. That I was invited to the opera house to hear John Philip Sousa's band."

Lottie cast a wry look. "Did you tell him you were going with an older man who had once been your mother's love interest?"

"Lottie Bell Foster! That is not one bit nice. They were only fifteen. Too young for anything serious."

Lottie was undeterred. "When you think about the situation, don't you think it's odd?"

Addie finished tying the bow in her hair. "I don't think about it. I need to talk to Alex. He's the one who chose the place. He could be my father and I could be his daughter."

"Only he isn't and you're not. Addie you said you had only met him once, but I think he is interested in more than finding out what your concerns are with Mrs. Tygert. Why else would he come out here?"

"How should I know. Maybe he needed a vacation. Lottie, stop. You are going to have me so upset I'll fall down the stairs."

Lottie laughed. "I know I'm not going to sleep until you get home and I hear all about him… John Philip Sousa, that is."

221

Addie picked up her gloves and gave her friend a slight tap on the shoulder. "Thanks for making my skirt. I love the way it sounds when I move."

"Don't spill anything on it. Taffeta will stain," Lottie cautioned.

Addie gave one last look in the dresser mirror. "I had better go downstairs and wait. Lottie, this isn't any fun at all. I have no thoughts on how to carry on a conversation with this man. I am a jumble of nerves."

"You have lots to talk about: Clay, the farm, Berryville, Tilly Stiles."

A smile creased Addie's face. "Don't you ever get flustered?"

"Not when there isn't any reason."

Addie was half-way down the stairs when she heard the rap on the door. She hurried the rest of the way and opened it to find Alex standing there. He was dressed as he was on the depot platform. But, she spied black trousers and spit-shined shoes and knew Alex Lockwood was dressed for a night at the opera house. She was glad for the fur wrap as she allowed him to drape it over her shoulders. She pulled on elbow length gloves and declared she was ready.

"You look very nice," he said when they stepped off the porch. "I hope you don't mind walking. I didn't rent a buggy because I thought it might be a nuisance to park it."

"We don't have far to go and the evening air is refreshing." She smiled up at him. "When I came here three months ago, I thought the air too thin and felt like I was living in the sky. Now, I don't even notice it."

He held onto her arm as they walked up the unpaved street. "It is much different than our Virginia. Do you plan on staying here?"

"I haven't decided. I talked Lottie into coming with me for a year. After we started, I changed my mind and told her that I would buy her a ticket home anytime she wanted. She likes her job at the department store, and she likes Caleb, so maybe she will stay the year."

He guided her around the corner to walk on the board walk of Harrison Street. "And, what about you? Do you like your job?"

"I'm learning a lot about medicine. Clay writes that there is a School of Pharmacy at the university. I want to do something with my life, but I certainly can't afford to go to the university with the money I make."

They were near the opera house. "How close are you and Clay?"

"I was so happy to see him when he came back this summer. It had been ten years. He gave me the watch pin that I'm wearing for a graduation present, and we promised to write to each other once he was in Charlottesville and I reached Leadville."

Alex seemed to consider this before he said, "I'm just getting to know Clay. Although we are brothers, he's much younger than I."

"Yes, I know. I also know my mother asked you to tell him to stay away from me. My mother can be hard in her ways sometimes."

"I am sure your mother was looking out for your welfare."

They were greeted at the opera house by a gentlemen wearing a black suit, white shirt and black bow tie. "May I take your wraps?" He removed Addie's fur and took Alex's overcoat and hat to a cloak room, handing Alex a ticket with a number on it.

Addie was in awe of the grandeur of the place. Crystal chandelier gas lights hung from the cavernous ceiling. Theatrical wallpaper decorated the walls.

Alex touched her elbow. "Are you ready?" he asked.

"I'm speechless," she whispered.

He smiled. "I thought you should have at least one night at the opera house while you are here."

They went up the steps to the auditorium where an usher showed them to their folding iron seats covered in a plush red material. Addie could hear the swish, swish of her taffeta skirt and felt she was well-dressed for the Tabor Opera House.

Once they were comfortably seated, Alex said, "Now, you can tell me what brought me to Leadville."

Addie looked all around. Satisfied no one was going to hear their conversation, she leaned close and in a low voice said, "Lottie and I are worried that Tilly Stiles is trying to take over Mrs. Tygert's affairs."

"That's a strong accusation, Adelaide."

"I realize that. Why else do you think I would have contacted you if I didn't feel it was important?"

"Why me? Why not another lawyer?"

Addie confessed, "Because you are the only lawyer I know and you are not from here. And, because I thought you owed my mother something, and because we have no money to pay you."

The warm smile in his brown eyes was reassuring. "Those are valid reasons. Do you want to know why I came?" he asked.

This surprised Addie. She could only nod her head as she.hadn't considered his side of the story.

He took her hand in his. "If I had not had that engagement in Denver, I'm not sure I would have come. I thought you were in serious trouble, and, yes, I did feel I owed it to your mother to help her daughter; a final closing to an unresolved memory. I also did it for Clay. I know he cares for you. And, I came for myself. I'm not sure it was a wise idea to move my law practice to Berryville. I came here to clear my thoughts."

Addie squeezed his hand. "Alex, I'm sorry. I never considered your feelings when I asked you to come. How selfish of me!"

"We will discuss our troubles on the way home. For now, we will enjoy this evening as though we are the only two people in the world and push our cares away."

Adelaide slipped her hand from his and tried to relax in her seat

**

Lottie was sitting up in bed eating a cookie. "I heard the rustle of your skirt coming up the stairs. Hurry up and get ready for bed so you can tell me all about it."

Addie plopped on her bed and threw her gloves into the air. "It was simply grand. I felt like Cinderella going to the ball on the arm of her prince. The band was decked out in red military jackets, yellow-striped black trousers and brass buttons; their highly polished instruments glistened under the stage lights. Then their music of ballads and modern tunes lulled one into a mellow mood until the booming Sousa marches trumpeted throughout the place. Alex and I felt like marching all the way home." She left the bed and began getting ready to retire.

"I hope you weren't so enthralled you forgot to ask him about our concern for Mrs. Tygert."

"Alex said we need to be careful of what we say. He also said it wouldn't be the first time someone had tried to exploit an older widow who was left on her own."

Lottie smiled. "At least he didn't think we were a couple of fools."

"No." Addie pulled on her nightgown and sat on the edge of her bed. She lowered her voice above a whisper. "I told him Tilly's behavior at the Thanksgiving dinner was out of character for her. He said he wasn't fooled. Her bearing was too ridged and she had a critical look in her eye that made him uneasy."

Lottie sat up straight and wrapped her arms around her knees. "Wowie! What does he suggest?"

"He wants to come and talk to Mrs. Tygert on Monday while we're at work and Tilly is at school."

Lottie clapped her hands. "We couldn't ask for anything better. I'm going to sleep good tonight."

"So will I. Is Caleb coming by tomorrow?"

Lottie was nestled under the covers. "Yes. He wants me to go out to his diggings."

"Do you think Caleb would mind if Alex and I come along? He also wants to hear from both of us why we are suspicious of Tilly."

"I don't think Caleb would care. Is Alex coming by tomorrow?"

Addie pulled up her covers. "He said he would be here at ten."

"You sure accomplished a lot this evening," Lottie mumbled.

Addie gave a contented sigh. "I surely did."

Chapter 34

Laura Richards was up early preparing breakfast. The weather had turned cold. She wondered if Colorado was colder and if Addie was warm enough. She had thought a lot about her daughter. It was their first Thanksgiving without Adelaide and the whole family had missed her. With Addie's father's help, Laura had finally come to the realization that Addie was now a grown woman capable of making her own decisions. It was hard to let go. But the boys still needed a mother and Sarah Jane was just beginning her life.

The sad moods Laura had experienced were in the past. Alex Lockwood's return to the farm had stirred up memories she had repressed for so many years. The last time she talked to him was when he urged her to let Adelaide live her own life. At times, Laura had seen Alex on the farm, from a distance, without any pangs of remorse. Time has a way of healing. Alex had grown away from her as she had grown away from him.

She wondered what Addie was doing at this minute.

**

Addie and Lottie were getting ready to ride up on the mountainside. Caleb was waiting in front of the house in the loaned buggy. Alex was leaning on it talking to him.

"Let's take our heavy quilts," suggested Addie. "I don't want to wrap up in that old blanket of Caleb's."

"You were happy to use it for the picnic," said Lottie. "Are you afraid Alex won't think it is good enough? If I recall, the seedy blanket was left in the cemetery wrapped around those two hoodlums."

Addie stopped what she was doing. "I'm sorry, Lottie. That did sound snobbish, didn't it?"

"Yes, it did," Lottie agreed. "You seem to get rattled when Alex is around. He and Caleb look like they are enjoying each other's company. Forget Alex is one of the Lockwoods and loosen up. I want to have fun this afternoon. We'll have to work on that Christmas stuff when we return."

Addie took a deep breath. "You're right. I don't care for this uptight feeling."

"I've packed lunch. You carry the quilts, and we'll pretend Alex isn't old enough to be our father. We can just be our silly selves."

Addie laughed.

Alex met them when they came off the porch. He helped Lottie into the front seat and Addie into the back, where he took a seat beside her.

"You look like you're ready for the day with those warm quilts," he said.

"I want to be warm," replied Addie.

Caleb joined the conversation, "I'll start a fire in the cabin when we get there and we'll be warm as toast."

"That won't keep us warm in the buggy," said Addie. "I know it will be a cold ride home."

Alex kept his eye on the countryside as they rode. "Was it gold that caused you to leave Oklahoma, Caleb?" he asked.

"My pardner and I were ready for somethin' different and pannin' for gold sounded right good. Most of the gold has been played out. Now they're dredgin' for it. Gougin' is more like it. They leave more piles of sand and gravel than they get gold."

"Not a pretty sight," observed Alex. "What are your plans? Are you going to stay here?"

Caleb was thoughtful. "Ain't fer shur. My pardner went back to ranchin'. Said he'd rather punch cows in the hot sun than pan fer gold in the cold."

"I don't know which I'd prefer to do," replied Alex.

"I like horses," said Caleb. "There's plenty of 'em out here. If I stay, I might look into a job with trainin' horses. I'm good at that. "

Alex spoke. "We raise horses on our place back in Virginia. If you ever wanted to come that way, I can guarantee you a spot on the farm."

Caleb turned off onto the narrow lane that led up to his small mining camp.

He answered, "That's mighty nice to hear. I'll keep it in mind."

They reached his camp, which was more like a shack. "How about if Lottie and me go in and warm the place up. Addie, you can show Alex how pretty it is by the creek."

All four of them stretched and moved to loosen the kinks from the bumpy ride.

Lottie carried the lunch basket and Caleb went to get firewood.

"This way Alex. You're in for a treat," said Addie.

He came to walk beside her. "Caleb is quite interested in your friend."

"How do you know?"

"He told me. He seems to be a decent fellow."

Addie smiled. "I like Caleb. Lottie said all she wants to do is get married and raise a family. She was all set to marry that no-account Sam Purdy if he would ask her. That's one reason I wanted to get her away from Berryville."

He took Addie's arm as they climbed up the rise. "I hear he's a trouble maker. What was your reason for this adventure? I understood you didn't want to be a teacher."

On the top of the rise, they could see the gentle waterfall with a background of the snowy mountain peaks.

"Adelaide! This is heavenly. It is so quiet and peaceful, I could sit for hours."

"I could, too, if it wasn't so cold. When Caleb first brought us up here it was warm. The sound of the water falling over the rocks was so peaceful, I felt I could throw all my cares away and watch them bubble on down the stream."

He guided her to a large flat rock and they sat side by side. "You didn't answer my question."

Addie thought about it. "I'm not exactly sure why I came. Partly, because I wanted to see more of the country. Mostly, because I was afraid I would get trapped."

"Trapped? What do you mean by that?"

Addie sat with her arms wrapped around her knees. "Maybe it sounds uppity, but I don't want to get stuck in a tenant house slaving away every day. I want more in life. I haven't figured out what."

He sat beside her in a heavy suede jacket and homburg hat resting his arms on his bent knees. "I'm still trying to figure that out, and I'm thirty-four years old."

Addie chuckled and looked over at him. "Is that why you never married; because you couldn't figure out your life?"

He picked up a pebble and threw it into the water. "Could be. I plunged headlong into the legal business. I didn't have time for courtships. Besides, I never ran into anyone I wanted to marry."

"Including my mother?" she asked.

"We were young. Marriage was never a question."

Addie sighed. "I wish my mother had taken that money your family bribed her with and did something with her life."

He looked directly at her. "Those are not kind words, Adelaide."

"I know, but that's how I feel."

He tossed another stone. "Your mother could have continued her schooling and gone on to become a teacher with the money my parents gave her. She chose to get married instead."

Addie sat in silence while his reasoning settled in. It was like turning on a light. "I never thought of it that way. Of course she could have."

She turned with a wide smile. "Alex, you have lifted a burden from my shoulders. I have felt guilty ever since I refused to go to the normal school. My mother could have easily chosen another path."

He stood up and offered her a hand up. "See? I solved all your problems."

"Except for Tilly Stiles," Addie said.

"Did you tell Mrs. Tygert I wanted to come by tomorrow morning?"

Addie brushed off the back of her skirt. "Yes, she's all for it. She said to tell that nice young man she would have coffee and cookies ready for him. Ten o'clock."

"If what you and Lottie have told me is accurate, I think I have a good idea about what's going on."

Addie was miffed. "Why would we not report accurately?"

"For one reason, you don't like Miss Stiles, and for another, she may be right about Anna's mind slipping."

"Lottie and I are not the type to tell tales!"

"Don't get in a huff. I'll iron it all out."

233

"I hope you can." As they turned to go, she turned to face him. "Sorry if I sounded unkind."

"It is just that the situation has worried you." He guided her down the path. "Come on. Let's see if the lovebirds have warmed up the shack."

"They aren't lovebirds," she contradicted.

"I predict they soon will be," he joshed.

"Alex, before I forget. We have Christmas presents for our families. Will you carry them home when you go?"

"That depends on if they will fit into my suitcase."

She was pleased. "I promise they will."

Caleb had a hot fire in the fireplace and Lottie had spread lunch out on the small table.

Caleb greeted them, "Good yer back. We'll have to eat Indian style on the floor. I left the door open so we can see what we're eatin'."

"I'm starved," declared Alex. "Is that fried chicken, Lottie?"

"Fried chicken, boiled eggs, molasses bread and apple tarts."

Alex bit into a piece of chicken. "You could cook for me every day. This is great."

"Thank you. I do like to cook."

Alex turned to Addie, who had filled a plate and was lowering herself onto the floor. "Can you cook like this?"

"No," she answered. "I'm not good at cooking or sewing. Lottie is the expert in both areas."

Lottie giggled. "Don't believe her. She doesn't like to cook or sew. She'd rather read Zane Grey westerns."

"Which reminds me," said Addie. "I hope to get up to the Carnegie Library in town and find a couple of good books to read."

Alex slid down beside her. "I could go check out a couple for you while I'm here."

"Alex, would you? I work so much it's difficult to get up there."

"Better yet," he said. "Lottie, do they sell books at that department store where you work?"

"Leopold Goldman sells everything he can get his hands on."

"Good. I'll purchase a couple books for you, Adelaide."

"No. They are free to lend at the library."

"But, not easy to return if you are too busy to get there."

Their attention was drawn to the open door when they heard a soft mewing sound.

"Will you look at that!" said Caleb, who was seated on the floor close to Lottie.

A mother cat deposited two newborn kittens on the floor.

"I think she wants to come in where it's warm," Caleb said.

They sat still and watched as she carried the kittens one by one into a corner of the room where an old flannel shirt lay in a heap.

"Could be she smelled the chicken," offered Alex.

"What are you going to do with them?" asked Lottie.

"I'll let her stay in here. If they live, I'll have to figure out what to do with them."

"If they live?" asked Addie.

"There's plenty of night predators up here. I'm wondering if she wandered up from town. She don't act like a wild cat," surmised Caleb.

"Do you think we can take them back to Mrs. Tygert's shed? They would be safe in there," suggested Lottie.

"Maybe kill some of the mice that roam at will," said Addie.

Alex raised his hands. "Don't look at me. I can't take them to the Clarendon."

"Let's do it this way," said Caleb. "We'll leave them here. You gals check with Mrs. Tygert. If she's fine with it, I'll bring them down next time I come up here."

"What if they don't live?" asked Lottie.

"Your troubles will be over," said Alex.

Addie shook her head. "That's callous."

He offered a half-smile. "No, that's practical," he answered. "Got any more chicken, Lottie?"

**

The light was beginning to fade when they returned to Leadville.

"Would you like to come in for a cup of tea or coffee?" Addie asked the men.

236

Alex responded, "Thanks, but no. I need to get back to the hotel. I have to put papers in order before I talk with Mrs. Tygert tomorrow."

"When will you tell us what she has decided?" asked Addie.

"That will be up to Mrs. Tygert." He turned to Caleb, who stood holding the picnic basket for Lottie while she folded her quilt "Caleb, you have a nice place up there. Don't ever let go of it unless you tell me first. Thank you all for a most comfortable afternoon."

"Lottie, I'll meet you inside. Caleb will you stay for coffee?" asked Addie.

"I'd better get this rig back to my old friend so he'll let me borrow it again."

Addie went through the gate and into the house.

Caleb walked Lottie up on the porch. As he handed her the basket he leaned forward and kissed her. "I've been wanting to do that," he said.

Lottie cast a coy look. "I've been wanting you to do that," she replied. "In fact, I think you should do it again."

He laughed. "That would be my pleasure." This time his lips stayed pressed to hers a wee bit longer.

He touched his big cowboy hat. "Yes, ma'am," he said. "That surely was my pleasure."

"Will you be coming next Sunday?"

"Wild horses couldn't pull me away. Let's plan on spendin' the whole day together."

Lottie grinned. "I'll bring some more fired chicken."

The happy cowboy flew down the steps and hurdled the gate of the picket fence.

Lottie waved when he started off in the buggy. She had to smile. Yes, Lottie Bell Foster liked Caleb Dunn right fine.

Chapter 35

At ten o'clock the next morning, Alex Lockwood arrived at the boarding house run by Anna Tygert. He looked official with leather briefcase in hand. "Good morning, Anna," he tipped his hat.

"Alex. It is so nice of you to come. We shall have coffee and cookies in the dining room."

He hung up his coat and hat and followed the little lady to the table set with china cups and saucers and four different kinds of cookies on a raspberry-colored glass plate.

"I do my best to keep cookies in my cookie jar for the girls," she informed, which told Alex she had a fondness for her boarders.

"I'm sure all three of your young ladies enjoy treats from the cookie jar."

Anna lowered her voice. "Oh dear, no. Tilly doesn't know they are available at all times. It is a secret Addie, Lottie and I share. Tilly is very strict with her rules."

"Tilly's rules? Isn't this your home, Anna?"

She poured the coffee. "Yes, but when Tilly arrived it was easier to follow her wishes. I was almost at my wit's end when she came to rent a room. I looked upon her as a gift sent from above."

He smiled that reassuring smile that made others comfortable. "I believe Matilda said the two of you are like mother and daughter."

Anna was hesitant. "That isn't entirely true. I respect Tilly's sharp mind. It worries me that she has caught me doing forgetful things. It is frightening to think I might lose my mind."

Alex looked directly at her. "I must be honest with you. Addie and Lottie feel that Miss Stiles is not truthful with you. That is the reason I came. They think she is trying to get control of your affairs. Has she suggested this?"

Anna had to think this over. "I believe it is only out of the goodness of her heart. She has offered to handle all of my affairs, if I am unable to care for them."

"Have you heard her mention Power of Attorney?"

Anna thought again. "I believe she did say words something like that."

Alex sighed. "Do you understand what those words mean?"

"I assume that she could sign papers for me."

"Anna, a Power of Attorney gives the person who holds it the power to take over everything of yours."

"Do you mean like my china and silver?"

"I mean, your money, your bank account, your house and everything in it. Yes, including your china and silver."

The thought of someone owning her two most cherished possessions seemed to ignite a spark of life in Anna. "Well, that just wouldn't do."

"You do understand what I am saying?"

"How could I not? You have stated it clearly."

He smiled. "I also must tell you that Addie and Lottie do not think you are any more forgetful than any of the rest of us."

"They are sweet young ladies," she mused. "But, they haven't had the years of experience that Tilly has had." She added, "Tilly doesn't always approve of the girls. She wasn't pleased that I rented a room to them. Tilly said it would have been far better to rent the room to one more settled lady."

Alex reached for another cookie. "How do you feel about having Addie and Lottie here?"

She was quick to answer. "They are a joy. There is nothing like the exuberance of youth. Don't you agree?"

Alex was fresh off a day spent with three young people. "Anna, I will agree with you. I spent yesterday with Caleb, Addie and Lottie. It was the most enjoyable day I have had in a long time."

"And, you escorted Adelaide to the opera house on Saturday evening?"

He smiled. "Yes, I did."

"Isn't she a charming young lady?" she asked, with a twinkle in her eye.

"Most charming. Now, to get back to the reason I came."

241

"Oh my, yes. It is just like me to get off the track. Would you care for another cup of coffee?"

He shook his head. Alex shuffled papers. "First, if you have not made a will, you need to get one written."

"Those are the kinds of things Mr. Tygert took care of."

"He had a will?"

"It wasn't like Mr. Tygert to leave anything undone. Yes, I believe there was a will."

"Do you have a copy?"

This question flustered Anna. "Oh dear me, I must have something some place."

Alex remained a calming influence. "Perhaps you put it in a safety deposit box at the bank. Many people do that."

She clapped her hands together. "Of course. That's where it is. After Mr. Tygert passed I was told to put the will in the bank, and be sure I kept the key in a safe place."

"You know where to find the key."

"Certainly. I keep it in my jewelry box. I wouldn't misplace that any more than I would misplace my china or silver." Then she remembered. "But I did lose my silver spoon at one point."

Alex made a note on paper. "You never found it?"

"Yes, I did. Tilly found it in with my everyday spoons. You see? A case of my absent-mindedness."

Or a part of the game Tilly was playing.

"If you are willing, I would like to see the copy of that will."

"I don't mind. I'll clear off the table and you can come to the bank with me."

Alex pushed the papers into his briefcase and waited for Anna to clear the table and retrieve the safety deposit box key before they started off to the bank.

They walked to the American National Bank on the corner of 5th and Harrison Streets. The brick and sandstone bank was narrow and deep.

She was greeted by a teller. "Good morning, Mrs. Tygert. Have you come to make your weekly deposit?"

"No. I have come to check my safety deposit box. Mr. Jacob, this is my lawyer, Alexander Lockwood from Virginia."

Cy Jacob extended his hand and Alex gave it a hearty shake. "What brings you to Leadville, Mr. Lockwood.?"

"Mrs. Tygert," Alex responded.

His clipped reply let the teller know there would be no information exchanged. "Of course. I will have to get our vice president to accompany you to the deposit boxes."

Cy Jacob returned with Wendell Knapp. After a quick introduction and Anna's verbal permission to allow Alex to accompany her, they went to view the contents of her safety deposit box.

Alex reviewed the papers in the box and made notes. He told Anna he had seen what he needed. Anna locked the box and Wendell Knapp replaced the security box in its rightful place.

They returned to Anna's house and sat in the parlor.

She chose her favorite rocking chair. Alex sat across from her. He pulled out the notes he had made. "Mr. Tygert took good care of you," he said. "The will states that after you are gone, the remains of your estate will be left to the church. If, in the event you can no longer take care of your affairs, he arranged for you to be cared for in the church-run home in Denver. Also, in the deposit box there are bank notes, bonds and railroad stock. These are worth money and can be cashed anytime that you are in need of money."

Anna was speechless. "When Mr. Tygert died, I feared I would end up penniless."

"That is not the case. I suggest that you hire a local lawyer to help with your financial dealings. You must keep that safety deposit key well hidden."

"I will put it back exactly where I found it." Then she questioned, "But, Alex, what if I am getting forgetful as Tilly says I am?"

"That is why you need a lawyer who can give advice when it is needed. Above all, when Miss Stiles mentions taking over your affairs, you can tell her they are all settled. In fact, you don't need boarders."

She shook her head. "No, no, no. Then I would be lonesome."

Alex put his papers back into his briefcase.

"Why can't you be my lawyer?"

His smile was gentle. "Anna, I live in Virginia. You need someone close at hand."

"Oh, dear," she lamented. "Such is life. You and the girls. Do you think they will stay here?"

"That is a piece of advice I can't give you." He stood and prepared to leave.

"Have you seen what those two young women have made for Christmas? They are wonders, that is all there is to it."

If Alex was in a hurry to leave he didn't show it. "No I've heard about their efforts. I believe they have presents that I am to carry back home."

Anna bustled past him. "Come, you must see."

She showed him into the busy room where the items were stacked in neat piles. "I believe Caleb will be coming to take them to Leopold's department store."

A sea of red, green, white and cream invaded his eyes. A strong fire in the fireplace caused rhinestones and gold threaded cloth to glitter. Anna held up a tablecloth with matching napkins. "Isn't this beautiful?"

Alex looked around at the many items they had crafted. He inclined his head to the side. "They are a wonder," he said.

Anna showed him to the door. "Will you be coming by again?"

"I will have to get the presents the girls want me to take back to Virginia. I plan to leave on Wednesday."

"If you come by tomorrow evening after the girls get home, we would love to have you come for dinner."

"I consider that a stellar invitation. Please tell Addie and Lottie that I will be coming. What time shall I arrive?"

"Six o'clock...or thereabouts," she answered.

Alex turned and waved as he headed for the Clarendon Hotel.

Chapter 36

Wednesday morning Alex was sitting in a Denver & Rio Grande railcar on his way to Denver. From there he would be on his trip back to Virginia. The train ride would give him time to think.

The reason he had come to Leadville was to settle a debt he felt he owed Laura Richards, and he wasn't sure why. He had done that by relieving her daughter of the worry that any underhanded attempts by Matilda Stiles toward Anna Tygert were no longer a threat. Alex had found a reputable lawyer in Leadville who was willing, for a price, to assist the widow. Alex made an agreement with Anna and the lawyer to keep Alex informed of any and all transactions regarding Anna's financial and mental status.

When he had returned to get the presents, Anna told Addie and Lottie of the arrangement. Everyone was satisfied.

Addie was so grateful she had given Alex a warm hug.

With mixed emotions, the good-deed lawyer looked out the window as the train pulled away from the depot. Leadville wasn't a pretty sight in early December. When the train rounded a curve, allowing him a view of the magnificent peaks of the snow-covered Rockies, he felt a pang of remorse.

The last few days he had spent were like a catharsis of the soul, relieving him of the cares he had brought with him. At thirty-four, he was a well-respected lawyer known in the Washington circles. He had moved from the busy flimflam of that city to Richmond, a smaller city with Southern roots. Even Richmond became too busy for him causing him to move back to establish a law practice in his native Clarke County, in Berryville, the county seat.

Alex wondered what he was looking for. Being with young people made him realize what he had missed along the way. He left Berryville years ago. Why had he returned?

He thought of Caleb Dunn, the tall, lanky and carefree cowboy from Oklahoma who knew who he was. Alex thought of easy-going, plump and pleasant Lottie. At eighteen, her simple wants could easily be fulfilled.

Then he thought of Adelaide. She was more complicated. She was attractive, bright, and wanted more out of life; she wasn't sure what.

That was where Addie and Alex were the same. Both searching for something. But, unlike Alex, Addie was younger. Maybe she would find her dream.

Alex inwardly smiled as he recalled meeting her in the stables with Clay. He liked her smile, he liked her eyes, he liked what he saw. Alex knew why he had come to Leadville. He wanted to see Adelaide and find out her feelings for his brother, Clay.

Anna Tygert had described it so well; the exuberance of youth. Is that what Alex had missed in his years of striving to make a name for himself?

He was thinking of moving his law office once again. That was what this trip to Colorado was supposed to do, help him make a decision. It was to get him away from the everyday trials of life itself. He had done that, but plunged headlong into a more difficult situation to solve... Adelaide!

**

Addie sat on the edge of her bed. She had received a letter from Clay. Lottie had gone to the cinema with Caleb. It was unusual for them to go out on a week night, and there were still items to finish with the Christmas material. Lottie said that if Caleb wanted to take her to see a picture, she was not going to sit home and work on stuff for Leopold's store.

Addie thought she was right. She hadn't told her about the letter from Clay because she wanted to read it when she was alone.

November 25, 1915

Dear Addie,

I am at home in Berryville for Thanksgiving. There are no classes on Friday so I have four days I can spend on the farm.

Charlottesville is an attractive place even though the fall splendor has passed. I am keeping up my grades but my heart isn't in it. I know I need to get a degree in something. I am leaning toward the financial courses.

You have been in Colorado for three months. I wonder if you are happy you are there and if you still enjoy your work in the drug store.

Relatives and family were all here except Alex, but I am told he had to give a speech in Denver. You do remember Alex? I wasn't pleased when he told me I was to stay away from you. He explained that was your mother's wish. Still, I didn't like him ordering me around.

How is Lottie? It must be comfortable to have your friend with you.

I have met a couple of fellows to chum around with, but I have not found a girl who is worth looking at twice.

You are the girl for me, Addie.

May you have a memorable Thanksgiving.

I miss you,
Clay

She had been eager to read the letter. Why did she feel deflated when she finished? Did she remember Alex? How could she tell Clay she had spent much of the Thanksgiving weekend with him? How could she tell Clay that she was the one who asked Alex to come to Leadville? How could she tell Clay that she spent the most wonderful evening of her life with his brother?

Addie's emotions ran the gamut from elation to despair. She knew Clay liked her. She didn't know how much, but she didn't like his writing that she was the girl for him. She didn't belong to anyone. Alex had asked her how she felt about Clay. Did he know Clay's feelings for her? Thoughts muddled her mind.

"I wish Lottie would get home," she murmured to no one but herself.

Addie went to the kitchen and snared a cookie from the Teddy Bear cookie jar. She took a big bite and returned to her room to get ready for bed.

When she heard Lottie coming up the stairs, she opened the bedroom door. "I'm glad to see you. I have a letter from Clay."

Lottie sent a wry look. "And?"

"Wait until you hear."

Lottie grinned. "No, you listen first. She held up her hand to sport a ring on the fourth finger of her left hand. "Caleb and I are engaged."

Addie's mouth was agape. Lottie sat on the bed beside her. She showed Addie the ring. It was delicate with a tiny sandy-brown stone that looked like a rose. "Caleb said he will get me a decent ring when he can. This is a rose rock. He used to carry it for luck and his luck was when he found me. He had the jeweler fix it into a ring. Oklahoma is one of the few places you can find rose rocks."

Addie had recovered and hugged her friend. "Lottie, I am so happy for you. I like Caleb and I know he has had his eye on you since we met him. I didn't expect it this soon."

251

"You are no more surprised than I was. He said we won't get married until he has a proper place for me to live."

"When will that be?"

Lottie laughed. "I don't know, but I won't wait more than a year. Now you can tell me about Clay's letter."

Addie read it to her.

Lottie was thoughtful. "Alex is gone, Clay is in Charlottesville, and you are here. That's enough distance to clear your thoughts."

"I don't want to cause any trouble with the Lockwoods."

"Do you know what you need, Addie?"

"What?"

"An identical twin."

Addie groaned. "Lottie, you're no help. I'm going to bed."

Chapter 37

Lottie told Anna Tygert about the mother cat and kittens in Caleb's camp.

"Oh, my goodness!" exclaimed Anna. "To think they might fall prey to some animal up on the mountain. It breaks my heart. I still wonder what could have befallen my poor Teddy."

"We were hoping, if they're still alive, that maybe they could stay in your shed until they are old enough to be on their own?"

"A splendid idea. Of course."

Lottie should have posed the proposition after Tilly had left for school.

Tilly fumed, "What are you thinking of!" Her nostrils flared on her pinched face. "There will be no cats brought to this house!"

"They will be cared for in the shed," Lottie countered.

Tilly rose from her chair. "And the next step will be into this house. I think not!"

Anna remained seated and composed. "Tilly dear, I believe this is still my house and I will make the decisions."

Tilly Stiles stomped out of the room and slammed the door on her way out of the house.

All was quiet. Anna looked at the two young women who sat as statues. "Tilly is like a volcano," she said. "One is never quite sure when she will erupt."

"Mrs. Tygert," said Addie. "I was proud of the way you stood up to her."

"I believe I have you to thank for that. You were the one who brought Alex here. He has assured me that Mr. Tygert took care of everything for me so I have no worries. After Alex made arrangements with Mr. Seal, a lawyer here in town. I have someone close I can call upon if need be."

"That was kind of Alex," replied Addie.

"Once I was relieved about what might happen to me, I began to look at life differently. I do not have to depend upon rental income to keep going. I no longer have to tiptoe around when Tilly is present. You know that I don't like disagreements. Before you came, I allowed Tilly to have her way because it was easier. I believe she will turn around."

"Or move out," said Lottie.

Anna smiled. "I don't think Tilly has another place to go. Perhaps I was as much a godsend to her as she was to me."

Addie checked the watch Clay had given her. "We need to hurry, Lottie."

When they reached the Golden Eagle, Leopold Goldman was unlocking the door. Addie ran on ahead to Davis Drugs.

"Here just in time, Miss Foster," Leopold greeted her. "I won't have to subtract from your pay."

"You had better not, Mr. Goldman. I'm putting in a lot of hours with the material you didn't know what to do with. Caleb is going to bring the items down on Saturday so you have them to sell for Christmas."

Lottie and Addie had made bib aprons for themselves out of the red, green and white striped cotton cloth. It brightened their spirit as well as the skirt and waist they each wore to work.

At the drug store, the door was unlocked and the druggist was turning on a light behind his counter.

"That's a fancy apron you're wearing," said Bernie Davis, after Addie removed her coat and hat.

"Lottie and I made them. We also made some to sell at the Golden Eagle."

He chuckled. "That will warm Leopold's heart. I suppose he's going to pay you for them."

"No. Someone sent him a lot of Christmas material and he didn't know what to do with it. He let Lottie and me use some for ourselves. We've made a lot of Christmas things for him to sell."

"Good old Leo. You work to make him money with something he never had to put a penny into. Then he repays you by giving you material he got free."

Addie started to ready the snack bar. "I didn't think of it that way. Lottie made me a beautiful skirt and she's making a dress for Christmas. We couldn't afford to buy them."

255

"How about if I give you free pens and stationery and in return you do my books for me?"

Addie stopped to think about it. Somehow it didn't seem the same. "I have plenty of stationery. What if I do your books and you pay me a dollar and a half more a week?"

Bernie stopped to mull over that idea. "Let's give it a trial. I'll tie up the year at the end of December and you can take over the first of January for 1916."

Addie was elated. Not only would she be earning more money, but Bernie Davis trusted her enough to do his accounting.

**

When Addie and Lottie returned to the boarding house that evening, Anna gave Addie a letter with a Denver postmark. She wanted to tear it open but dinner was on the table and Tilly sat tapping her fingers.

Anna had fixed a pot of ham, potatoes and cabbage. The smell of freshly baked bread was still in the air.

"Tilly is prepared to say grace," informed Anna.

Addie and Lottie took their seats and waited for Tilly's order to the Lord.

For conversation, Anna said, "Tilly, our Miss Lottie is engaged to Mr. Dunn."

Tilly looked over at Lottie. "That's sudden, isn't it? You hardly know him."

"I know all I need to know," answered Lottie.

"I am very happy for her," Addie said. "Caleb is a thoughtful and caring man. He will be a good husband to Lottie."

"Don't be too sure. Men can be deceitful."

Addie felt Lottie bristle, so she injected, "I don't believe deceit is in character for Caleb. He is honest and forthright in his manner."

"What caused you to be so sour on life, Tilly?" asked Lottie.

There was a hush in the room waiting for her reply.

"Yes, I'm soured by life. You young women have your lives ahead of you. I am close to forty and my chances have passed. If you had grown up under my mother's rule, you would understand. I was afraid to go against her. She's dead and look where I've ended up."

"You have a respectable position and can take care of yourself," said Addie. "That is more than a lot of women have."

For the first time since they had arrived, the young women felt a pang of sympathy for Tilly Stiles.

"Don't you think I would love to spend a day as you four spent the day together on Sunday? It was clear all had a most enjoyable time. And, Adelaide, I envied you dressing up so prettily and going to the opera with Alex. Yes, it was pure envy. A cardinal sin!"

The three women sat still in the quiet room. They had heard Tilly's confession and were not sure how to answer or if they should answer.

Lottie was the first to speak. "Miss Stiles. You are too hard on yourself. There are many widowed men who would be grateful to have your company. Maybe you should relax your rules for yourself and allow them the chance. You should practice smiling."

This must have struck a note with Tilly because the faintest of smiles was evident.

Tilly rose from her chair. "Anna, thank you for the meal." Then she turned to Lottie. "Thank you for the advice."

Addie and Lottie helped clear the table, except for the china and silver.

Anna offered, "I have cinnamon buns for dessert.

"None for me," said Addie.

"Lottie, it looks like it is up to the both of us to indulge."

"I'm all for it," said Lottie.

Addie pulled the letter from her pocket and tore open the envelope on her way up the stairs. The note with the Denver postmark was from Alex.

Dear Adelaide,

I am sitting in the Denver depot waiting for my next train. I couldn't leave without telling you what a good time I had in Leadville. As I had said, I needed time away from my daily routine for insightful thinking. I believe I am on the right track.

Thank you for contacting me. If you hadn't, I would still be in a stir.

I trust you will find what you are searching for, and I hope it will be soon.

You, Lottie, and Caleb made me feel young again. The day we spent at his camp was carefree and eye-opening. The night at the opera house was sheer bliss. You were a lovely companion.

Please write to me in Virginia to tell me how things are going for you.

I am sending you my love,
Alex

Addie lay back on the bed. I am sending you my love? What did he mean by that?

Chapter 38

On Saturday, Leopold allowed Lottie to leave early so she could meet Caleb at the boarding house to load in the Christmas items she, Addie, and Mrs. Tygert had fashioned. Leopold loaned her crates to haul them to the store.

When they arrived at the house, Anna was waiting and watched as Lottie and Caleb loaded the colorful articles. "I almost hate to see them go," she said. "They brightened the room and the work kept me busy."

Lottie thought it was right to take the remnants back to the store because there was still enough material to make a few things. They had two weeks before Christmas.

At the Golden Eagle, Leopold ordered two of his clerks to help unload the buggy and place the articles in a corner of the deep store.

"What's this stuff?" he asked, pointing to the box of remnants, and chewing on a cigar at the side of his mouth.

"It is the material that's left over. We didn't have time to use it all," explained Lottie.

"Not going to store that. You got use for it?"

Lottie answered right away, "I do."

"Good. Have your young man load it right back into that poor excuse for a buggy."

This time Leopold Goldman had gone too far. Lottie was piqued. "Mr. Goldman, you owe Caleb an apology. We didn't ask you to rent a buggy or pay someone to haul these free pieces to your store. Caleb did it because I asked him to. If you wanted what you would call a respectable buggy, then you could have let go of your tight-fisted money, rented one and paid someone to do the labor!"

The three clerks in the store stood dumbfounded.

Leopold stood looking at his outspoken employee. Lottie looked right back. He took the cigar from his mouth. "You're absolutely right," he said. "I apologize young man. That was thoughtless of me. No excuse, no excuse."

Lottie's ire had simmered. "Mr. Goldman, this is Caleb Dunn. We are to be married."

"Miss Foster, you are full of surprises." Leopold shook Caleb's strong hand. "You are lucky. Lottie is a talented young lady and an asset to my store."

"Yes, sir," Caleb answered. "I am lucky, and I do accept your apology."

"You're not going to drag her away from here too soon, I hope."

"Not for a while," said Caleb.

In a brighter tone, Lottie suggested that Leopold check the goods they had brought.

He was almost rubbing his hands with glee after he reviewed the array of items. Most likely he was contemplating the income they would bring.

"We'll make a spot right near the front where everyone can see them."

Lottie held a satisfied smile.

When they were through at the store, Caleb suggested that they go to check on the cat and kittens up at his camp. Lottie was for it, but first she needed to stop at the drug store and tell Addie so no one would be worried if she wasn't home at dinner time.

Addie said she would tell Mrs. Tygert when she arrived home. Addie still had another hour to work.

Bernie Davis peered over his work counter. "That your friend who's engaged?"

"Yes, that was Lottie."

"When are you getting married, Miss Richards?"

"Not for a long time!" she answered.

Bernie laughed. "Don't let life pass you by."

Walking to the rooming house, Addie pondered Bernie's words, "don't let life pass you by." Is that what happened to her mother, to Tilly Stiles, to Alex Lockwood?

Once inside the house, Addie removed her heavy coat and navy cloche hat. She shoved wool gloves into her coat pockets, then went into the dining room.

"Lottie will be coming later. She and Caleb went up to check on the kittens."

"It is a cold evening to be out," said Anna. "I do hope she has a warm wrap."

"I'm sure Lottie is prepared," answered Addie. But Addie wasn't sure. Lottie's head was still in the clouds over her engagement.

Tilly said grace in almost a sincere tone. In fact, she was cordial throughout the meal talking about her day at school. Was this a new Tilly? Was it because Lottie was absent?

It was close to eight o'clock and Addie was beginning to worry. Lottie wasn't home yet. Addie looked out the small bedroom window at the peaks of the Rockies. The moon was in its crescent phase. Addie whispered a silent prayer.

By nine o'clock, Addie was sitting by the fireplace in the living room. The mantel clock struck nine times. She counted each bong and hoped for the door to open. But the door didn't open. All was quiet inside and outside the house.

Later, she heard the clop, clop of a horse and the gritty sound of wheels on gravel. Addie ran to the door and threw it open to the cold air. Caleb was helping Lottie down from the buggy.

"Lottie!" exclaimed Addie. "I have been so worried about you."

"She needs to get in where it's warm," said Caleb. "We were comin' back down and the wagon slid on ice throwin' it off the lane into the stream runnin' next to it. Lottie got wet tryin' to help me get it straight."

"I'm all right, Addie. Caleb's worried because we're so late."

"That ain't true. You can catch a bad cold."

263

"Look, Addie. We got the kittens. The momma cat was gone."

Wrapped in the flannel shirt that had been their home in the cabin, Addie peeked in and saw four little eyes staring up at her.

"Caleb took two baby bottles filled with milk just in case we needed them. I don't know how long their momma has been gone, but these two were hungry. It was good that we went up tonight."

"Lottie, you need to get into the house."

They heard Anna Tygert call from the doorway, "Is everything all right? Is that you, Lottie?"

"Yes, it's me."

Next they heard, "What is all that racket? I have school tomorrow!"

"Caleb and Lottie have brought the kittens. There was an accident with the buggy, but everyone is fine," Addie called back. "Lottie, you get inside!" she ordered.

"Bring the kittens inside," called Anna. "It's too cold for babies to be outside."

"I knew it!" scoffed Tilly.

They made their way to the porch. Inside, Caleb stood on the stair landing, not wanting to mark the floor with his wet boots.

Addie went upstairs with Lottie to get her into some dry, warm clothes.

Anna took the kittens. She and Tilly unwrapped them to find two furry little bundles. "Meow."

Anna marveled over them. "Look Tilly, this one looks just like my Teddy."

The other, a calico, brushed Tilly's hand as she opened the flannel shirt and continued to rub against her trying to find the warmth of her skin.

"I think that little one likes you, Tilly."

"They're goin' to need to be hand-fed for a bit 'cause their momma's gone," said Caleb. "Do you want me to find a place fer them in the shed?"

"No," answered Anna. "They're too little to be out in that cold."

"I got two baby bottles I can leave."

"Bring them in," said Tilly.

She turned to Anna, "You're not going to be able to feed them both tonight. I can take this one to my room. When it is old enough, it can go to the shed."

Caleb brought in the bottles and asked them to tell Lottie he had to be on his way.

When Addie and Lottie came down the stairs, Caleb was gone and the two women were holding the kittens.

"I am taking care of this one," explained Tilly, "until it can be on its own. Anna will feed it when I'm at school."

"They aren't going to the shed?" asked Lottie.

Anna answered, "Oh, dear, of course not. I believe these are a gift from above."

Tilly looked at Lottie. "You had better drink some chamomile tea. You look bedraggled. And, put a teaspoon of honey in it," she added.

Tilly picked up the calico kitten and the baby bottle, which now contained frozen milk, and headed upstairs.

Lottie looked at Addie," What got into her? I thought she hated cats."

"I don't know," said a bewildered Addie. "Maybe she'll strangle it."

Lottie laughed. "Now you sound like me."

"Come on. You need to have that tea."

Chapter 39

Three days later, Lottie was in her sewing room at the Golden Eagle. She hadn't felt good since the accident with the buggy.

Leopold Goldman stuck his head inside the door. "Are you all right? You don't look so good."

Lottie coughed before she answered. "I can't say that I feel great."

"You go ahead and go on home and get some rest. You worked hard on getting all that Christmas stuff together and the stuff is going like hotcakes. Too bad you couldn't have time to make some more."

"But, I have some alterations that need to be done by next week."

"I got a woman in town can do that kind of work. You get on home because you look pale around the gills."

This was Leopold's way of saying he cared.

Lottie didn't have to be told twice. She put on her coat, hat, and gloves, picked up her pocketbook, and left the store. The walk home felt like it was miles away. By the time she reached the rooming house, she could barely make it up the stairs.

Anna Tygert came up to their room. "I thought I heard one of you girls come in," she said. "What is the matter, Lottie dear?"

"I am sick."

Anna came into the room and felt Lottie's forehead. "You're burning up. You need some aspirin and a cold cloth for your head."

Anna hustled out of the room.

Fifteen minutes later she carried a tray containing tea, aspirin and a chunk of ice wrapped in a washcloth. Lottie swallowed the two aspirin with a drink of tea and placed the cold cloth on her forehead. She had never felt so bad.

When Addie arrived home, Anna hurried to meet her. "Lottie is very sick," she said.

Addie rushed up to their room where she found Lottie with a flushed face and mumbling incoherently.

"Lottie, it is Addie."

"Mama?"

Addie took her hand in hers. "No. I'm Addie."

Lottie coughed and opened her eyes. "Addie, I think I'm dying."

"You're not dying. You are very ill."

"I thought I was home on the farm. Everything swirled around in my head: Pa, Mama, the farm. I even saw Clay riding a horse. My head hurts so much, it feels like it will explode."

"You need a doctor."

"No. I'll take more aspirin. Can you bring me some ice for my head?"

"I'll be right back," answered Adelaide.

Anna was in the kitchen. "You haven't eaten your dinner," she said. "How is Lottie?"

"When did she have aspirin?

Anna stopped to think. "It must have been around two o'clock. Right after she came home."

"Then I can give her some more. I'm also going to put ice in tea and more ice for her head. Mrs. Tygert, if she isn't better in the morning, I am going to get the doctor."

Addie placed items on a tray and hastened back up to where Lottie lay on her bed in the cramped room. She helped her best friend raise her head enough to take the pills and swallow the cold tea.

The next morning Addie was tired. She hadn't slept except for a few snatches in-between administering to Lottie, who was no better.

Even Tilly was concerned. "I heard her thrashing about during the night. It must have been the accident the evening they brought the kittens home."

"I'm getting the doctor right after I go to the drug store to tell Mr. Davis that I will come in later. There's a doctor's office on my way. Mrs. Tygert, will you keep an eye on Lottie while I'm gone?"

"Of course I will, dear."

Addie gulped down what was left in her coffee cup and grabbed a cookie to eat on the way. She hadn't eaten dinner last evening and her stomach was not pleased.

Bernie Davis understood Addie's need to be with Lottie. He told her to take the day off.

"Mr. Davis, thank you so much. If Lottie improves, I will come back this afternoon."

"No you are to take the day. You look tired."

Addie almost ran to the doctor's office. She had not met the physician and prayed he would be kind enough to come quickly.

She entered the office where a young man sat at a desk. "I need to see the doctor," she said.

He smiled. "That would be me."

The only doctor she had known was Doctor Hawthorne in Berryville. Addie thought all doctors were older with graying temples and a portly bearing.

"You're too young," she blurted out.

"They didn't think so in medical school."

Some men keep the look of a teenager into their twenties and he was one of those men. His blue eyes twinkled. "I am new in town," he said.

"So am I," said Addie. "Well, not too new, I've been here almost four months."

"What brings you in?" he asked.

Flustered and embarrassed, Addie tried to act calm. "It is my friend. She is very sick."

"What seems to be the problem?"

"She has been burning up with fever to the point of being out of her head."

"Does she have a cough?"

"Please, come and see for yourself. I am overly worried about her."

270

"That's evident. I'll get my bag and you lead the way. Is it far?"

"No. A few blocks."

He locked the door to his office and turned a sign that said, "Back in an Hour".

They reached the house. Addie made a quick introduction of Doctor Robert Nelson to Anna Tygert before she hurried him up to their room.

"It's cozy," he remarked. He had to walk sideways between the beds and duck his head. "Hello, Lottie," he said, as though he had known her for years.

Lottie groaned.

Doctor Nelson opened his satchel and took out a stethoscope. "When did you say she had that accident?" he asked Addie.

"About four days ago."

"Did she bump her head?"

"She didn't complain about any problems, but Lottie is not a complainer... not much, anyway."

When he finished his examination, he motioned to Addie to follow him. They reached the parlor. "Your friend has pneumonia and possibly a concussion. She needs to go to St. Vincent's Hospital where the nuns can take care of her."

Addie had to recover from his words. Her mind was in a tizzy. "Nuns?" asked Addie.

"Yes, the Sisters of Charity run the hospital."

All of this was news to Adelaide. She had heard of nuns but she had never seen one. Certainly not in Berryville.

Medicines for the hospital were provided by Davis Drug, a man came to pick them up and deliver them. Addie was never interested enough to inquire about the hospital.

"Can't I take care of Lottie here?"

"She needs twenty-four hour care, especially for a few days until the pneumonia begins to clear, if it does."

"If it does!" Addie didn't recognize the high pitch of her voice.

He placed a reassuring hand on her arm. "I need you to understand how sick your friend is. She is young and healthy. I believe with around the clock care, she will have the best chance."

Addie was close to sinking. The good doctor guided her to a chair. She choked back tears and said, "I want what is best for her."

"I'll arrange for her transfer," he said.

As soon as Robert Nelson was out the door, Addie flew up the stairs. She tried to be matter-of-fact. "Lottie, the doctor says you need to go to the hospital for a couple of days."

Lottie's voice was weak, but she didn't protest. "I have to work."

"We'll worry about that later. I'll talk with Mr. Goldman and get the news to Caleb."

Lottie tried to smile. "Not very good news, is it?"

Addie hugged her friend. "We will get through this."

**

That evening Addie lay awake. How had her world crumbled so fast? Christmas was two weeks away and there was no joy. Caleb had not taken the news well and blamed himself for the folly with the buggy. Addie blamed herself for talking Lottie into coming to this place awash with gamblers, drunks and tarts. Unpleasant thoughts filled her mind.

In the morning she was still tired. What little sleep she had was not restful. Addie not only worried about Lottie but about the money they didn't have. Both had managed to put some money back. It would be used up in a flash.

On her way to work, Alex came to mind. She would call him so he could tell Lottie's parents. If the phone operator on duty in Berryville was one who would carry gossip, the whole town would know. She had to risk it. Did she dare reverse the charges again? She would risk that also.

On her break for lunch, Addie hurried to the Mountain States Telephone and Telegraph office. The long distance operator placed the call and Alex accepted. With a sense of relief, Addie heard, "Alexander Lockwood."

"Will you accept a long distance call from Adelaide Richards?"

"Yes."

"Go ahead," said the operator.

"What's wrong, Addie?" he asked before saying hello.

"Alex, Lottie is in the hospital."

"Are you all right?"

"I'm tired and worried."

"I understand," he said. "What does the doctor say?"

"He hopes she will recover in a few days."

"Can you discuss this over the phone?"

"No, Alex." Addie didn't want Lottie's parents to know how sick she was and cause undue worry.

"I'll see that her parents get the news as soon as I get back to the farm."

Addie gave a sigh of relief. "Thank you. How are things at home?"

"Getting ready for Christmas."

"Will Clay be coming home?"

"I suppose," he answered.

His terse reply was unexpected. "Thank you again," said Addie.

"You're welcome... Adelaide, it's nice to hear your voice."

"Goodbye, Alex."

Addie hung up the receiver. It was good to hear his voice, too. She was glad she had called; the day didn't seem so despairing.

After work, Addie went to the hospital. Caleb sat next to Lottie's bedside holding her hand, a concerned look on his face.

"Hi Caleb. Is she better?" She moved to the bedside.

Lottie tried to open her eyes. "You're blurry."

"You recognize me. You must be better."

"No. My head throbs."

A nun came in with a dose of medicine. She wore a long white dress and a headdress that looked as though she could fly up into the sky. She smiled at the visitors but she was all business. The spoonful of medicine was followed by sips of water.

"That's bitter," complained Lottie. And she drifted back to sleep. The good sister smoothed the sheets before she turned and left the room.

Addie placed a hand on Caleb's shoulder. "Caleb, I'm happy you're here. I'll stop by tomorrow. There is no use for me here unless you want me to stay."

"You go on ahead. They won't let me stay past eight o'clock," he said. "I'm worried, Addie."

"We all are. Send up a prayer."

"I ain't good at church stuff."

"Do you believe in God?"

"Yes, ma'am."

"That's all prayer is, talking to God about your troubles or thanking Him for the good things that come your way."

Caleb grinned. "Shucks, I've done that plenty of times."

"I'll see you tomorrow," she said and left the room.

The hospital was a wooden structure with two wings. Addie didn't like the smell. It was a mixture of food, cleaning solutions and people. She

275

took a deep breath in the mountain air when she left.

Anna Tygert had left a roast beef sandwich and boiled egg, in the kitchen for Addie. She poured a glass of milk from the icebox. Her mind recalled the events of yesterday and today. Addie wasn't sure why she felt better, but she did. Maybe it was talking to Alex on the phone. It gave her a sense of being home.

**

By the end of that week, the doctor said Lottie showed some improvement, although it was nothing Addie could detect. Robert Nelson was fresh out of medical school. Addie hoped he knew what he was doing.

He told Addie and Caleb that he thought Lottie had hit her head during the accident which would account for the severe headaches. The blurred vision and fever were gone. The cough was worse, but he said that was good for her to cough up the phlegm.

When Addie went to the hospital, all she could do was sit and watch Lottie's labored breathing until a spasm of coughing woke her.

Caleb was dutiful in his attendance. Sometimes Lottie seemed to sense their presence only to drift back into slumber. If a fit of coughing gripped her, both Caleb and Addie would be on edge until it passed. There was nothing Addie could do or say to ease Caleb's anxiety. After five days both were beginning to wear down.

Addie went home before Caleb left the hospital. She hated to walk by herself in the dimness of the evening. On one corner there was a saloon, so she crossed the street before she reached that spot. She could hear the raucous music and loud voices laced with profanity. As long as no one was lounging outside of the place, she felt safe. To her way of thinking, law enforcement was lax in Leadville.

She went up the steps of the rooming house. It was late and the house was quiet. A shaded light was on in the parlor. Addie hung up her coat, then unpinned her hat and placed it on a shelf.

"Hello, Addie."

She jumped and let out a cry of surprise. "Alex?"

He rose from the easy chair and came to meet her.

"What are you doing here?"

"I thought you could use a friend. You didn't tell me anything but I understood from the tone of your voice that it was serious. How is Lottie?"

That was when Addie broke down in tears.

Alex put his arms around her and led her to the chair he had just vacated. He handed her a handkerchief. "Not good news?"

Addie wiped her tears and blew her nose. "Alex, she is so sick. The doctor says she is holding her own, which doesn't sound encouraging to me. Caleb is lost."

He sat on a footstool next to her. "Tell me what happened."

Addie related the whole tale of the accident, bringing the kittens here, and that Lottie and Caleb are engaged to be married.

"I was sure that would be the case when I left. That's good news, Addie."

"I can't get it out of my head that she might die."

He took her hand in his. "Let's erase that thought right now. You said the doctor has seen improvement."

She sniffed and wiped her nose again. "How did you get in?"

"I knocked on the door. Anna and Tilly were having dinner. Anna fed me and invited me to wait here until you came home. Addie, after you called me I knew conditions were grave. I made the fastest connections I could. Lucky for me the trains were almost all on time and I had no holdovers. Five days. I still feel like I'm riding a train."

Addie squeezed his hand. "I'm so pleased you came. Did you tell Lottie's parents?"

"I did. I didn't know how sick she was, just that she was in the hospital. I told them I assumed it was a bad cold."

Addie thought about it and nodded her agreement. "There was no reason to worry them."

"You look worn out Adelaide. Have you had dinner?"

"No. Mrs. Tygert has been leaving food for me."

He stood up and pulled her to standing. "Let's go raid the kitchen. Are you feeling better?"

"I think I needed a good cry and a friend to share it with. I thought you said you had dinner."

He led her out of the parlor. "I did. Anna made the best fried chicken. I was too polite not to make a pig of myself. I'm hoping there are a few pieces left."

Indeed, Anna had left fried chicken and rolls. They ate what they could along with a cup of tea Addie brewed for each.

While they sat eating, there was mewling and scratching at the kitchen door. Addie opened the door and in ran a cat. "That looks like the momma cat from Caleb's place!" she exclaimed. "How could it get here?"

"Smelled the fried chicken," kidded Alex, and he threw a piece to the cat.

"That can't be the same cat. How is it possible she could get all the way here?"

"I suspect she followed the scent of her kittens. I've heard stories that cats travel for miles following a scent."

The cat was oblivious of the two humans as it busily devoured the chicken Alex had thrown to her.

"She looks like she's been in a war," observed Addie.

"She must have had a rough trip."

"Do you think she'll go into the shed?"

"She's hungry and there's chicken left. I'll entice her with it."

Alex dragged the chicken in front of the cat. Addie unlatched the shed door while Alex encouraged the scraggly cat out of the kitchen. He threw the piece of chicken inside the shed. They quickly closed the shed door. "Momma Cat" was secure for the night.

Addie was hopeful. "Mrs. Tygert threw that old flannel shirt in there that the cat used for a bed in Caleb's camp. Maybe she'll find it."

Alex smiled. "If not, she is set for the night. You hurry back inside before you catch cold."

"I hope we haven't woken Tilly. I'll hear about it in the morning."

They went back into the kitchen. "Guess what," she said. "Tilly has adopted the calico kitten and keeps it in her room. She named it "Rainbow". I still think Tilly had a hand in Teddy's disappearance."

"Teddy?" Alex raised his eyebrows.

"That was Mrs. Tygert's cat. Caleb picked it out of a tree once and he disappeared a few days later. That was before we came. Mrs. Tygert was crushed."

"Has "Rainbow" sweetened Matilda's disposition?" he asked.

"I feel sorry for Tilly at times. Life hasn't been all that pleasant for her."

Alex replied, "I have decided that life is what we make it. I plan to start living as I should have about ten years ago."

Addie laughed. "Ten years ago I was almost nine years old."

"Ten years ago, I was almost through with the study of law and determined to make a name for myself. Well, I did. Now, I'm going to start over."

A wistful look graced Addie's face. "I wonder where I will be in ten years."

Alex was putting on his heavy overcoat. "I hope you're not in Leadville."

"Are you going to see Lottie tomorrow?"

"That's my plan. I have some business to discuss with Caleb."

"Business with Caleb?" she questioned.

"I'll tell you about it tomorrow. What time are you off work?"

"Five-thirty."

"I'll meet you at the drug store. And, Addie, I am taking you for a decent meal."

"Coming out here is costing you a lot of money, but I am very glad you came. I feel so much better."

His words were sincere. "When I spent the time here at Thanksgiving, it was a turning point for me. I had to come. Tomorrow at five-thirty?"

"I'll be waiting."

This time it was Addie's turn to watch Alex walk away.

Chapter 40

Addie was counting the minutes until she was through for the day. She wore a long-sleeved white blouse and plain navy skirt. Wherever Alex decided to eat, her dress would be respectable.

At five-twenty, he came into the drug store. Addie was waiting on a customer so he browsed the shelves.

When she was free, Addie walked over to him and said, "Come and meet Mr. Davis."

Alex went with her to where Bernie Davis was cleaning up his work space.

"Mr. Davis, this is Alexander Lockwood, a friend from Virginia. He came to see Lottie."

Bernie wiped his hand before extending it to Alex. Bernie Davis," he said. "Nice to meet you."

Alex offered the smile that warmed his brown eyes. "Adelaide tells me that you have been helpful to her."

"I thank the day Miss Richards walked into my shop," he said. "Will you be in town long, sir?"

"My reason for coming is to check on our mutual friend in the hospital, and I have business to clear up. If Miss Foster is recovering well, I assume I will only be here for a day or two."

"Good to have you in town," said Bernie. "You go ahead, Miss Richards. I'll close up."

There was snow on the streets. Addie didn't want to wear galoshes because they would be too cumbersome. She had oiled her ankle-length leather boots and hoped that would be enough protection from the wet snow. She couldn't afford to ruin her shoes, but she didn't want to look like a farmer clomping down the street.

"Do you think Caleb will be at the hospital?" asked Alex.

"He said he usually makes it in by five-thirty."

"Good," he answered. "I did go by this morning. Lottie was sleeping. One of the nuns was coming out of her room, and mentioned the doctor was pleased with her progress."

Alex took her arm as they crossed Harrison Street.

"I'm glad he is. I wish I could understand what he sees to be pleased about. She is pale and has lost weight."

Alex chuckled. "Maybe that's not so bad."

Addie sent him a disgusted look. "Just because Lottie is a little overweight doesn't mean you can make fun."

"I'm sorry. I'll make it up with a wonderful dinner at the restaurant next to the Clarendon."

They reached the hospital and, as expected, Caleb was sitting at Lottie's bedside. With an astonished look, he rose when they came into the room.

His voice was almost a whisper. "I'm right surprised to see you," he said as he shook Alex's hand. "I thought you were back in Virginia."

Alex matched the low pitch of Caleb's voice. "I was. Addie called to tell me Lottie was in the hospital so I came right back."

"That's a mighty long trip," said Caleb.

"It is," agreed Alex. "I came for another reason. I'd like to take you and Addie to dinner so we can discuss it."

"They boot me out of here at eight o'clock. I couldn't go before then."

"Sure you can," came Lottie's weak voice.

Addie ran to the bed. "Lottie, you're awake."

She coughed and Addie held a glass of water to her lips to ease the irritation.

"Go Caleb. I can't talk without coughing. You can use a good meal."

"You haven't been this awake since you came in here," said Addie.

"I'm supposed to be better." This time her spasmodic cough caused her to put her hands to her chest, beads of perspiration broke out on her forehead. When it was over, she lay back on the pillow. Lottie raised a hand. "Hi, Alex. Take them both away. Let me die in peace."

"Lottie Bell Foster! Don't you talk like that!" exclaimed Addie.

Lottie turned her head and smiled at them. "Doctor Nelson says I'm going to be fine. It will just take time."

"Now, Lottie, you never told me that," said Caleb.

"I like that worried look on your face," she answered and coughed again. "Go get a decent meal."

Addie squeezed her hand and Caleb kissed her on the cheek before the three left the hospital for a well-deserved dinner.

Addie was happy to see the restaurant was not classy. It allowed her and Caleb to feel comfortable. Had Alex taken that into consideration?

Alex said he had made a reservation. The adjoining tables were not in earshot as the reserved table sat in an alcove. The waiter showed them to their spot and seated Addie before the two men took their seats.

Alex said, "A brandy for each of us to take off the chill."

The waiter left menus and went for the brandy.

"I have never had brandy," admitted Addie.

"A sip at a time," advised Alex. "It will warm you to your toes."

Caleb smiled. "It will do that for shur."

Alex took charge. "Look over the menu and decide so we can give the waiter the order when he returns. I'd like to get on with my purpose for coming."

The brandy arrived and the waiter took their orders. When he left, Addie watched as the two men sipped their brandy. It didn't look difficult so she put the glass to her lips and demurely took a taste.

285

It burned all the way down! Tears came to her eyes as she stifled the urge to cough.

"Alex smiled. "What do you think?"

She cleared her throat and tried to talk but her throat was tight and constricted. She waved away his question until she felt she could answer. "They could use this for embalming fluid."

Alex laughed. "It is warming, is it not?"

"I will grant you that," she said.

Alex addressed Caleb. "Do you remember me saying that you could have a spot on the farm?"

"I do."

"I have bought a big place on the other end of the county I live in and I need someone honest to run it. My plans are to raise horses and cattle, no dairy cows. You've been a ranch hand. I thought of you right away."

Caleb sat without speaking. Finally, he said. "I'm right pleased that you asked. That's a big job. I don't know. I know horses and cattle, but I've never been that far east."

"I don't need your answer tonight. I will be buying stock in the spring. I want you to think it over. When Lottie feels better, talk it over with her. I hear you two are engaged."

Caleb grinned from ear to ear. "We are. No weddin' date yet. I'll be honest with both of you. Lottie being so sick has made me think that maybe we shouldn't wait. I'm not shur what I'd do if I lost her."

Lottie married? The thought struck Addie with a jolt. That would change everything. Lottie wouldn't be there to share their room or share their secret thoughts or snipe at Tilly Stiles. Addie would be alone.

Adelaide placed the napkin, awash with red and white poinsettias on her lap. "We have to get Lottie well first."

She held up the napkin she had just unfolded. "Someone has been shopping at the Golden Eagle. Lottie and I made these."

The waiter came with their dinners: lamb chops for Addie, steak for Caleb, and pork loin for Alex.

They stood in front of the restaurant after dinner was over. Caleb told Alex he would think about his offer and bid them goodnight.

Addie and Alex turned in the direction of the rooming house.

"What did you think of my offer?" he asked.

"Why did you buy your own farm? I don't see how you can run a law office and a farm at the same time."

"I don't plan on running it. If Caleb is as good a man as I think he is, he'll be able to hire the right people and oversee the place."

"What about all the bookkeeping that goes with it? I don't think Caleb is up to that."

Alex didn't answer right away. He picked up a handful of snow, made it into a ball, and threw it as far as he could. "You could do that, Adelaide."

She stopped in her tracks. "A bookkeeper on a farm? I don't think so."

He laughed. "Come on, just a thought. You said you were doing the books for the drug store."

"I will be. That starts in January. I might not be good at it."

"The owner wouldn't ask you if he didn't think so. You said you were tops in your class."

"Second," she corrected.

He made another snowball and threw it at a snow-covered bench. "Which means you have a good brain. All I want you to do is think about it, Addie."

"Is that the real reason you came?"

"Partly. I was concerned about Lottie, I wanted to pose the possibility to Caleb, and I wanted to see you. Not necessarily in that order."

Addie smiled. "I am glad to see you. Lottie kidded me about going to the opera with a man sixteen years my senior. I didn't feel that way. In many ways it seems we are closer in age."

He reached for her gloved hand. "Do you mean, I act younger or you act older?"

"I don't know. I only know that I am comfortable when you're around. It wasn't that way at the beginning. I kept thinking about you being my mother's old boyfriend. Something changed after I got to know you."

"Adelaide, I wish you would get that out of your mind. I look at it exactly the way it was. An infatuation when we were fifteen."

288

They were almost to the rooming house. Alex still held her hand. "When I left here, I had to search my mind as to how I could change my life. The opportunity to buy the farm came up and I jumped at it. I will be my own man, a new start owning something I can grow into something even better."

"It took you thirty-four years to figure that out?"

"No, only the last few. I enjoyed what I had accomplished. I closed up my practice in Richmond and came home to sort out my life. You know the rest of the story."

They walked up the steps to the porch.

Alex said, "I'll check in on Lottie before I go. In fact, I'll write out what is involved if Caleb decides to take the job. There's a nice house on the property they could live in and I'll pay him a god salary. I'm excited about this venture, Addie. Think hard about being a part of it."

Addie felt a pang of sadness. "Are you really going so soon?"

"I probably should have stayed in Virginia and waited for word if Lottie was getting better. I came because I was concerned about you. If something happened to Lottie, you would be alone. I didn't want to think about you being out here by yourself."

Addie took his words to heart. "You have been very good to me. Maybe whatever I am searching for will drop out of the sky and I'll know what I want."

"I hope so," he said and kissed her cheek. "Goodbye Addie."

"Goodbye, Alex."

He gave a gentle squeeze of her hand and turned away.

She wanted to cry and wasn't sure why. Alex Lockwood had struck a nerve.

Chapter 41

Lottie was released from the hospital the day before Christmas. Caleb picked her up in the loaned buggy that had started the whole ordeal. He brought a heavy quilt and wrapped it around her after she was seated. Lottie carried a basket of fruit that Leopold Goldman had sent. After being in the hospital for almost two weeks, it was good to breathe fresh mountain air.

Addie and Anna were waiting at the rooming house when Caleb pulled up. Addie ran out to meet them. She hugged Lottie. "It is so good to have you back. Don't you ever give me a scare like that again."

"I'll do my best not to," said Lottie.

Caleb carried the basket of fruit. "Lottie says this is for all of you," he said. Anna directed him to put the large package on the sideboard in the dining room.

The basket not only contained fresh and dried fruit but hard candies and nuts, also. Anna pressed her hands together as she admired the contents. "This is wonderful for Christmas. With Lottie being home, we are going to have a grand time. Come for dinner tomorrow, Caleb. We eat at two."

"Yes ma'am," he said. "I'd be proud to come."

Addie wanted Lottie to go to bed and lie down. Lottie had other ideas. "I have been in a bed for days. Let's sit here by the fire and talk about Alex."

Anna Tygert brought in tea and cookies. "Here is a little something for you girls. How are you feeling, Lottie?"

Lottie smiled. "I will be fine once I get my strength back. I have missed your cookies."

"These are fresh out of the oven. A warm molasses cookie will cheer you right up."

Lottie chuckled. "I know it will."

Anna went about her tasks, and Addie poured tea from the fancy china teapot. "What about Alex?" she asked.

"He came by the hospital before he left. Doctor Nelson was there and Alex heard him assure me that I would be fine. Alex left information for his offer to Caleb, Do you know what he offered?"

"No, he didn't get into details."

Lottie leaned forward in her chair. "One thousand dollars a year, plus a house for us to live in."

"A tenant house?"

"It would be for five years. If the farm thrives under Caleb's care, we can buy the house and fifty acres for a reasonable price. Addie, it is something to work for."

"What does Caleb think about it?"

"He said we couldn't ask for a better start. You know I want to go back to Virginia."

Addie sighed. "I know. You weren't all that crazy about coming out here. When you got sick, I kicked myself for pushing you to come."

"If I hadn't, that would have been my loss. I found Caleb out here. Mrs. Tygert would call it a gift from above."

Addie laughed. "That's what she thinks about the kittens. She calls hers, "Angel".

Lottie giggled. "Aren't angels supposed to be dressed in white? Her kitten is orange with white spots."

"Mrs. Tygert says that angels come in all colors."

"Addie, I know I promised you a year. Caleb plans on taking the job Alex has offered, and he thinks we should get married before he gets settled there."

Addie wasn't surprised at Caleb's decision to take the job. She was surprised that Lottie would not be going with him. "I thought you would leave when he does."

"As Alex is planning on starting to buy stock in the spring, Caleb plans to arrive there in February. That will give him some time to get used to the area and the plans Alex has for the place. If that works out, I will join him in April."

"When are you getting married?"

"Just before he leaves. He said we'll have our honeymoon when I get to Virginia. I can't go to his rented room and he can't come here and the cabin isn't fit. We don't have the money to rent a hotel room."

Addie felt bad. "If I had the money, I would give it to you."

"Don't look so downcast. You know I don't ask for much. If I have Caleb, I will be more than happy to wait for a honeymoon."

Addie shrugged. "Have you told Alex?"

"No. And you are not to tell him either."

Lottie had finished her tea and two molasses cookies. "I'm going up to lie dawn. Don't let me sleep through dinner."

Addie held a pleased look. "I promise. Mrs. Tygert and Tilly are going to Christmas Eve church services. We'll have the house to ourselves. I wonder what is going on at home tonight? Christmas Eve was always hurried with last minute preparations."

Lottie gave a sideward glance. "Don't you mean, what is Alex doing? He and Clay are probably in a fistfight over you. I wasn't fooled that Alex came to see me or Caleb. He was concerned for you, Addie."

A contemplative sigh escaped. "Alex asked me to be the bookkeeper on the farm he's bought."

Lottie hesitated for Addie to offer more information.

"Did you hear me?"

Lottie nodded. "What are you going to do?"

"I don't know. I wish I was more like you. You know what you want out of life."

"Addie, you knew you didn't want to be a teacher. You knew you didn't want to end up in a tenant house. You knew you didn't want Clay. You don't know about Alex."

"How do you know I didn't want Clay?"

"Because you would have found any way to meet him behind your mother's back."

"I like Clay," countered Addie.

"You like Clay but you don't love Clay. You don't know how you feel about Alex because he is older, because he is Clay's brother, and because of your mother's teenage infatuation. Are you afraid of what people will say?"

Addie had to think about it. "I'm afraid of myself. I don't want to make a bad decision, Lottie."

"You aren't pushed into making any decision. You're going to start taking care of the bookkeeping at the drug store and that is all you have to be concerned about now. You will either like it or know that kind of business is not for you. No one knows what the future holds."

Addie had to smile. "You are a wise woman."

"With that bout in the hospital, I grew up a lot." Lottie stood up. "I am wise enough to know that I need to lie down." Up the stairs she went.

Chapter 42

December was over and January was hurrying along. The holidays had been quiet. There was a big New Year's Eve dance in town. Neither Addie not Lottie felt like going. Lottie wasn't up to it and Addie wouldn't go by herself, so Caleb came over and they spent the evening playing cards with Anna Tygert. She had made popcorn balls and a pan of fudge. The whole town was liquored up with various forms of alcohol. The only spirits in the Tygert house were the four people sitting at the table. Even Tilly went out to celebrate the coming year at a fellow teacher's home.

Addie had received a letter from Clay. He wrote that he had spent Christmas at the farm. He and Alex had a talk. He knew Alex had asked Addie to take care of the bookwork at his new farm. Clay wondered if she had made any plans. Addie had not written back. She wasn't sure what to say or what Alex had told him. Had he told Clay about their night at the opera? Their time at Caleb's camp? Or that she was the one who had contacted Alex? Not once, but twice? It wasn't right not to tell the whole story. But, Clay hadn't written anything except about the bookkeeping.

Alex had written, also. He was elated to hear that Caleb accepted the job and would arrive in Clarke County in February. The timing was perfect for allowing the new foreman to get settled before he began his duties at the farm. Alex was doubly glad Caleb and Lottie would be married before Caleb left Leadville. As a wedding gift, he had sent a check. Caleb used the money from that to reserve one night at the Clarendon Hotel. A one-night honeymoon satisfied Lottie.

**

Addie closed the books for the week.

"Got big plans for tomorrow?" asked Bernie Davis, peering over his work counter.

"As a matter of fact, I do. My friend, Lottie, is getting married. Caleb will be leaving next week."

"He's that cowboy from Oklahoma," he said as more of a statement than a question.

"Yes. Do you remember Alexander Lockwood, our friend from Virginia?"

"He had a nice way about him," said Bernie.

"Alex has bought a big farm and Caleb is going to Virginia to run it."

Bernie came around the corner of his work area. "That means your friend will go with him. What are your plans?"

She put the ledger in its rightful place. "Lottie won't be leaving until April. Caleb has to get everything settled first."

"Adelaide," he dropped the formal Miss Richards. "If you plan to follow, I want to know ahead of time because I will have a time replacing you. You have this store running like a clock."

Those words caused a pang of concern. Was she getting like Tilly Stiles?

Addie put on her coat. "I have no plans. First, I am going to enjoy Lottie's wedding. I'll see you on Monday, Mr. Davis."

**

The Justice of the Peace arrived at Anna Tygert's rooming house fifteen minutes ahead of schedule. Anna led him into the parlor where Caleb, dressed in a freshly laundered plaid flannel shirt, string tie, and polished cowboy boots paced the braided rug. His neatly combed sun-kissed hair shone in the firelight.

The dining room table was covered by a white linen tablecloth. In the center was an arrangement of dried flowers in a silver bowl. Crystal candlesticks with tall creamy tallow candles sat at each side of the bowl. The sideboard contained Mrs. Tygert's coveted china and silver.

Addie and Lottie were upstairs in their crowded room. Leopold Goldman had given Lottie a bolt of cream-colored satin. She didn't have time to make an elaborate dress, but the drape of the satin was elegant. Lottie wore the gold locket her parents had given her for graduation. She fashioned a circular headdress of satin, ribbons and dried flowers.

Addie stood back to admire her friend standing in the hallway. She felt happy and sad at the same time. Her best friend was starting on a new adventure, and Addie was losing her closest ally.

"What's that?" whispered a startled Lottie.

They stood perfectly still and heard the strums of a guitar playing "Here Comes the Bride". Lottie raised her eyebrows, shrugged her shoulders. "Let's go," she said.

They came down the stairs. Addie was dressed in the outfit she wore to the opera and a slimmer Lottie, who had not regained the weight she lost when she was ill, came down the stairs behind her.

Tilly Stiles stood in a corner of the room playing the guitar. Life is full of surprises.

Caleb wasn't sure who to ask to be his best man. He couldn't very well ask the old miner who loaned him the well-used buggy, so he asked Robert Nelson. He was the doctor who had pulled Lottie through her illness with a mixture of creosote and iodide, a cure for pneumonia he had read about used by an island doctor. Dr. Nelson was more than glad to accept the duty.

After the ceremony and the justice had left. Mrs. Tygert and Tilly put on a scrumptious dinner.

The physician brought a bottle of champagne, which none of them had ever tasted, but by the time dinner was over and the three-tiered wedding cake was served, they were all in a good mood. Even Tilly Stiles tittered away.

Caleb and Lottie climbed into the rented buggy, courtesy of Leopold Goldman, and headed in the direction of the Clarendon Hotel amidst handfuls of rice thrown by the happy onlookers.

Anna and Tilly insisted that Doctor Nelson needed to be introduced to their kittens. Whether he liked kittens or not, he was polite and pretended they were delightful; maybe he was truthful.

He told them that his betrothed from Omaha would be arriving next week. This wedding was a good primer he'd said.

Addie helped clean the remains of dinner and had another piece of cake. Tilly finished the few drops of champagne. In a light mood, the three women retired for the night.

Addie had been alone when Lottie was in the hospital, but tonight was different. She and Lottie would never share the room as the soulmates they had previously been. Marriage changed a lot of things.

Chapter 43

Addie penned a letter to Clay.

March 1, 1916

Dear Clay,

I have neglected to write to you because I wasn't sure how to form the words.

Two months ago you asked if I had made a decision about taking the bookkeeping position at the farm Alex bought. I wasn't sure, then. Today I am certain that I will.

Lottie was married in January. That event had an impact on my life and forced me to look at the future. I will be returning home older and wiser in these few short months, although I feel I have been away from my home for years.

I cherish the watch pin you gave me for graduation and I would be lost without it.

I must tell you that your letters lead me to believe that you are expecting that we will have a relationship other than friends. That cannot be.

There is a school called, Katherine Gibbs, where they train women in secretarial and accounting skills. Alex is willing to pay my tuition. I, in turn, will take care of his farm finances.

I am not sure what you and he discussed at Christmas. Alex has made the long trip out here twice, at my bidding. I am not sure what would have happened if he hadn't come.

In April, I will come back to Clarke County with Lottie. She and Caleb will be living on the farm. I will return to live with my parents.

Keep up your studies at the university. I now understand why my mother pushed me to do my best.

Your friend,
Addie

Addie hadn't written to Alex. She had called him on the phone to tell him of her decision and paid for the long distance call herself. A letter was less expensive than a phone call, but she wanted to hear his voice. He had accepted her decision with cheer and relief.

Leadville was cold, cold, cold. Snow still fell and ice still formed. At times the mountain passes were clogged. It had been that way since before Christmas. Caleb was in Virginia and Lottie was counting the days until she would join him.

Alex had written to Addie. He said the house was ready for Lottie and Caleb. Hired help stayed in the big house, which had been thoroughly cleaned. As Addie would be his bookkeeper, she needed her own space. Three rooms had been set aside for her until her training was to begin at Katherine Gibbs School.

As for Alex, he lived in town during the week and visited the farm on weekends. He was overjoyed to see everything falling into place.

Addie was happy that she didn't have to return to live with her parents. In April she would be nineteen and a woman on her own.

Addie had done deep digging into her thoughts. Alex was willing to pay the cost of tuition for one year at Katherine Gibbs. She would have further education that would serve her well. She would never get trapped.

Alex said he would benefit because he would get a highly trained secretary and bookkeeper.

Most of all, once she finished her training, Addie would be working closely with Alex and the thought pleased her. As Lottie Bell Foster had started a new phase in her life, Adelaide Mae Richards was embarking on a new course.

Her decision to come to Leadville had been a good one. She felt certain her plan to return to Clarke County was just as good. Addie had resolved any guilt she felt about not going to the State Normal School. As for Clay, what was it Lottie had said? "You like Clay, you don't love him." She was right. It wasn't the same with Alex. Addie knew she held deep feelings for him and hoped his were as strong for her.

She recalled the words he had written when he first left Leadville on his return to Virginia. "I am sending my love." What did that mean?

Of course she knew!